IRON MAN™

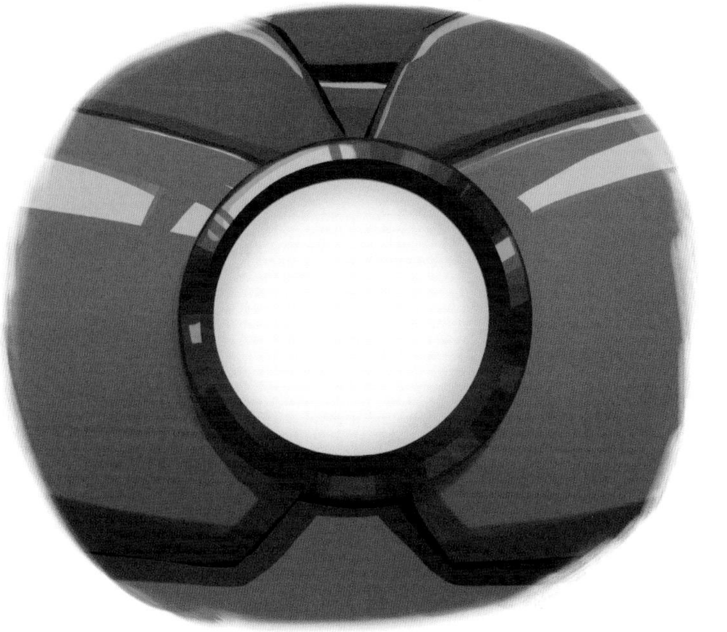

AN ORIGIN STORY

Based on the Marvel comic book series Iron Man

Adapted by Rich Thomas Jr.

Illustrated by Tom Grummett *and* Hi-Fi Design

MARVEL
New York

TM & © 2013 MARVEL & SUBS.

Published by Marvel Press, an imprint of Disney Book Group. No part of this book may be reproduced or transmitted in any form or by any means, electronic or mechanical, including photocopying, recording, or by any information storage and retrieval system, without written permission from the publisher. For information address Marvel Press, 114 Fifth Avenue, New York, New York 10011-5690.

Case Illustrated by Pat Olliffe and Brian Miller
Designed by Jason Wojtowicz

Printed in the United States of America
Second Edition
1 3 5 7 9 10 8 6 4 2
G942-9090-6-11227
ISBN 978-1-4231-7253-6

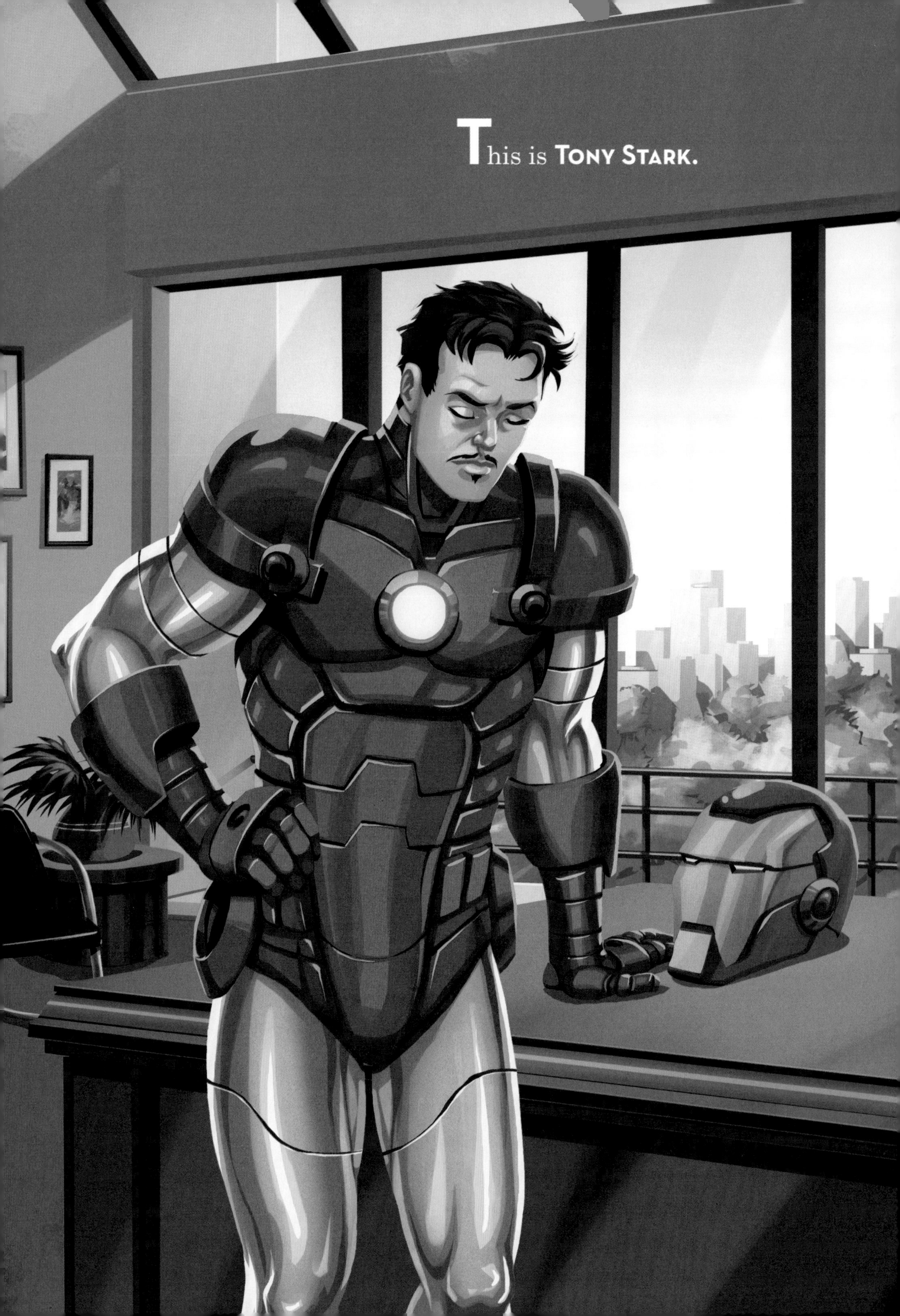

This is **TONY STARK.**

Tony is usually as regular a guy as you or me

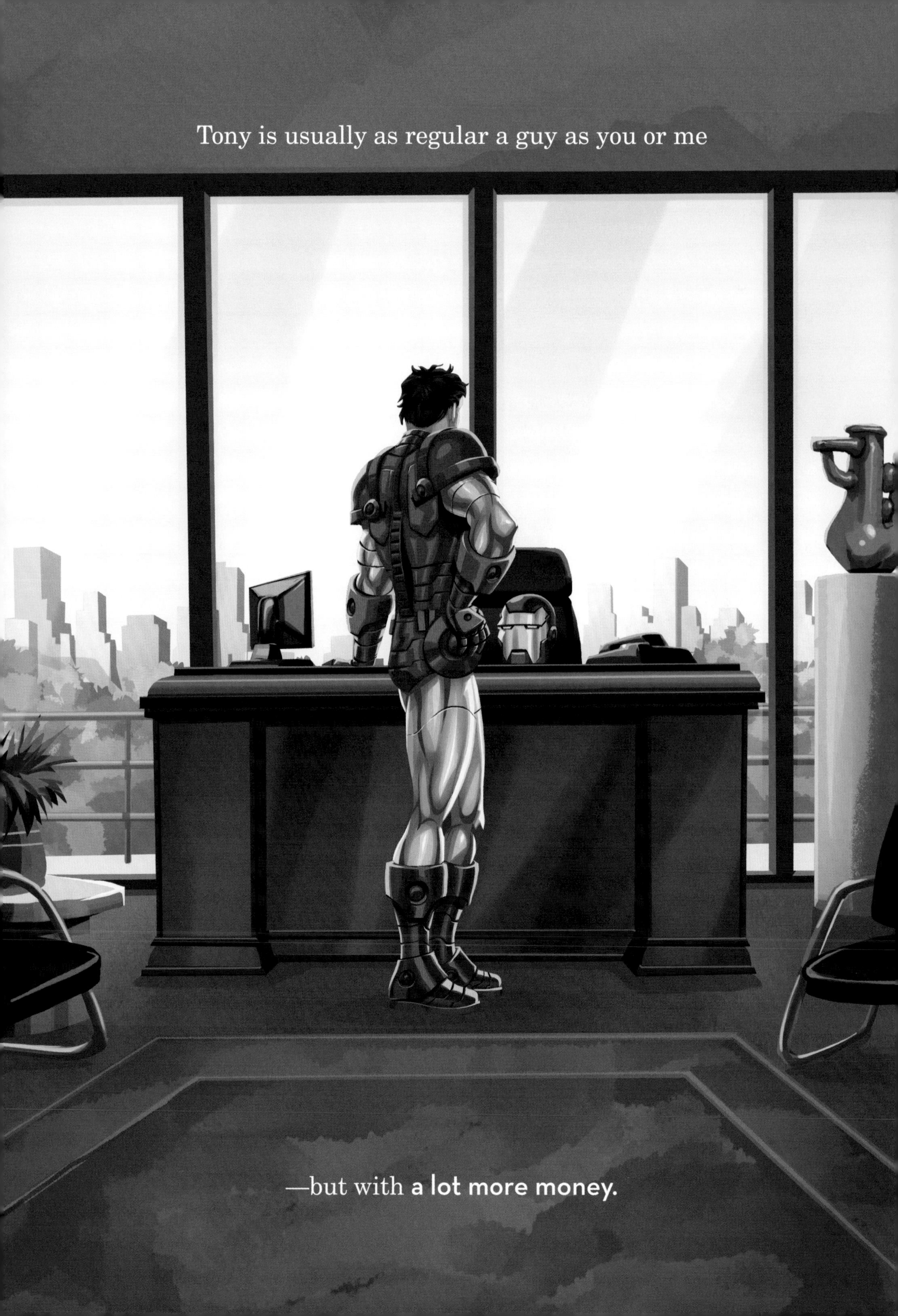

—but with **a lot more money.**

When Tony puts on his special armor, he becomes more powerful than most people. He even calls himself something different.

When he puts his armor on, Tony is . . .

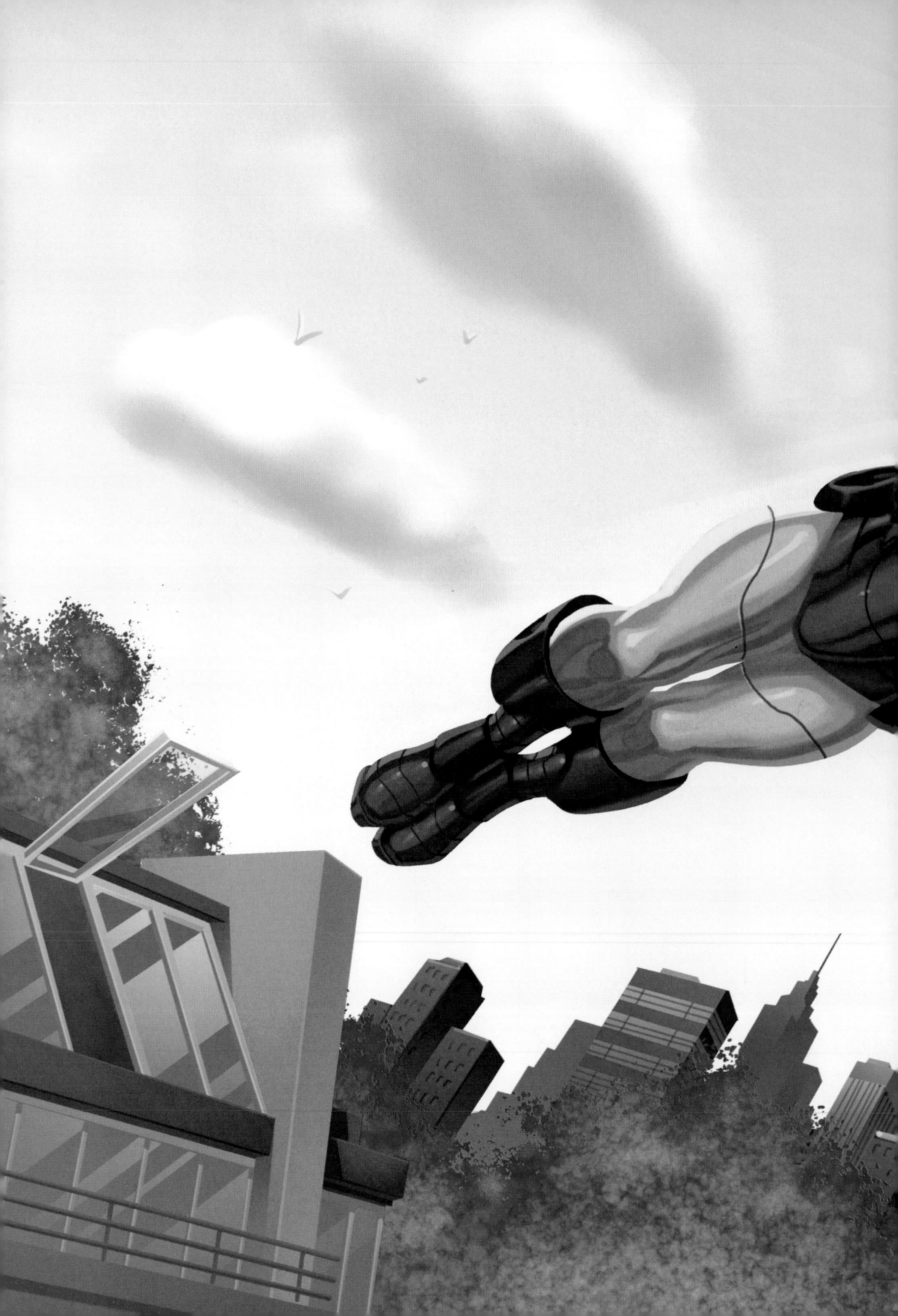

THE INVINCIBLE IRON MAN!

But Tony wasn't born a Super Hero.

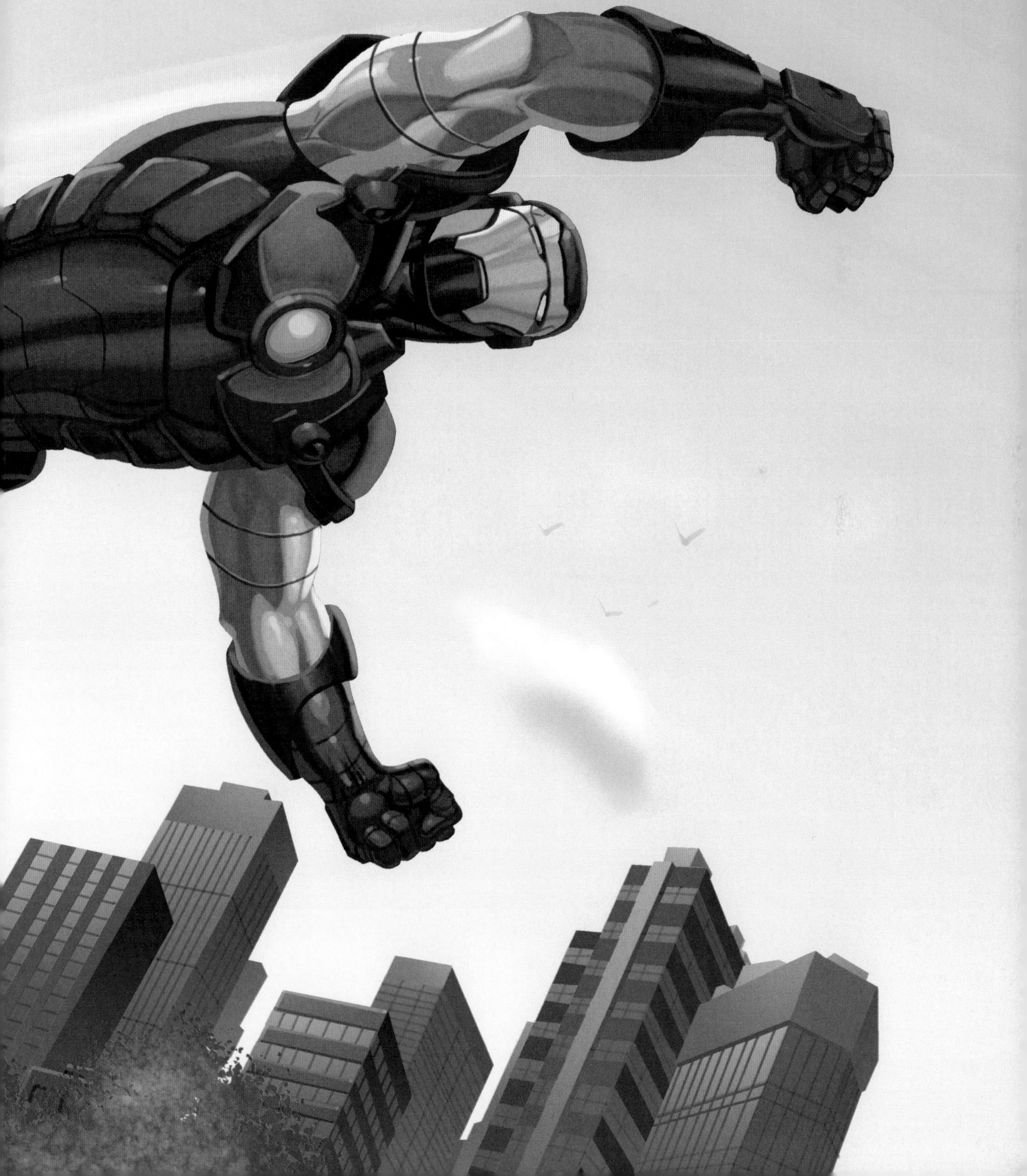

He hasn't always fought to protect people.

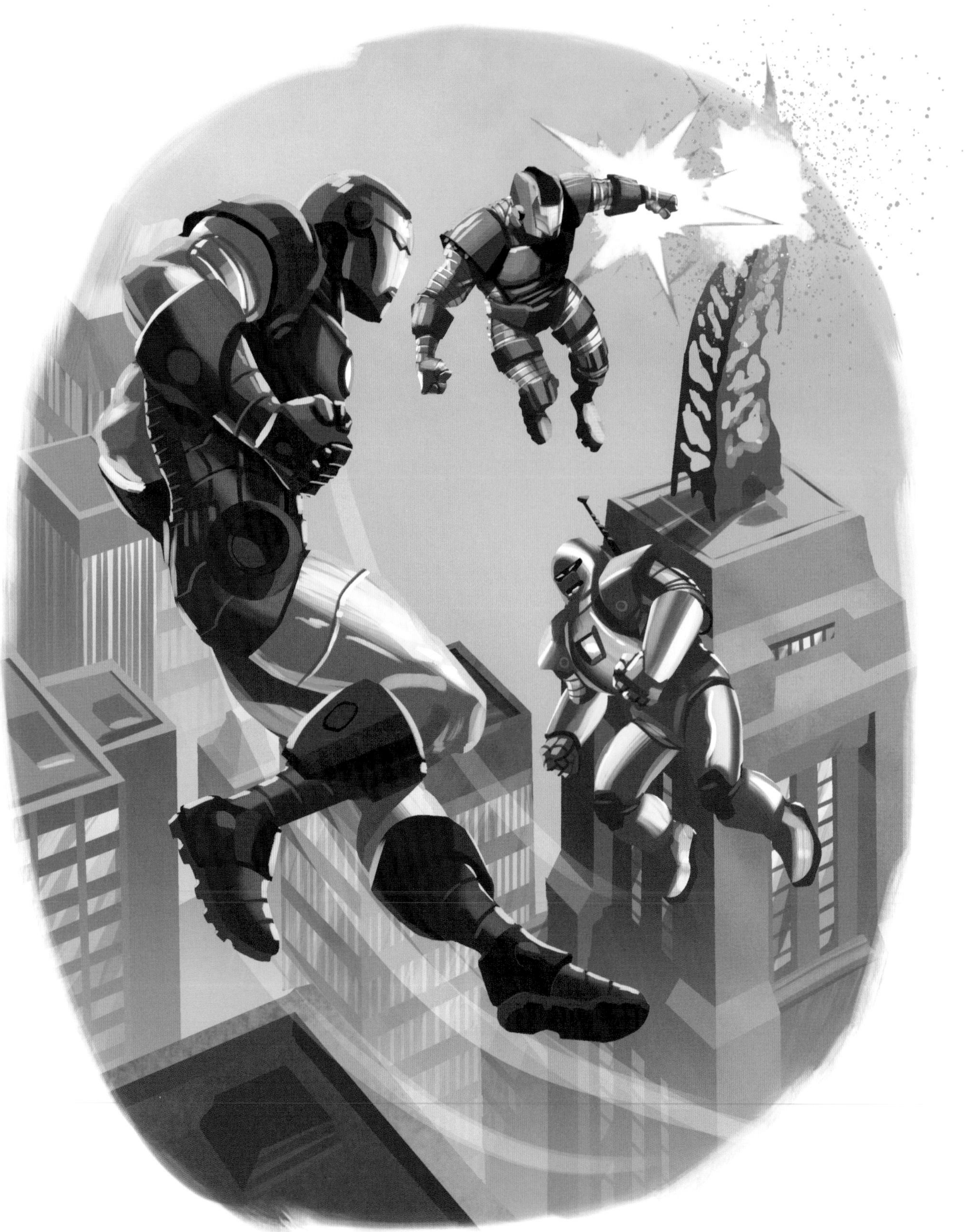

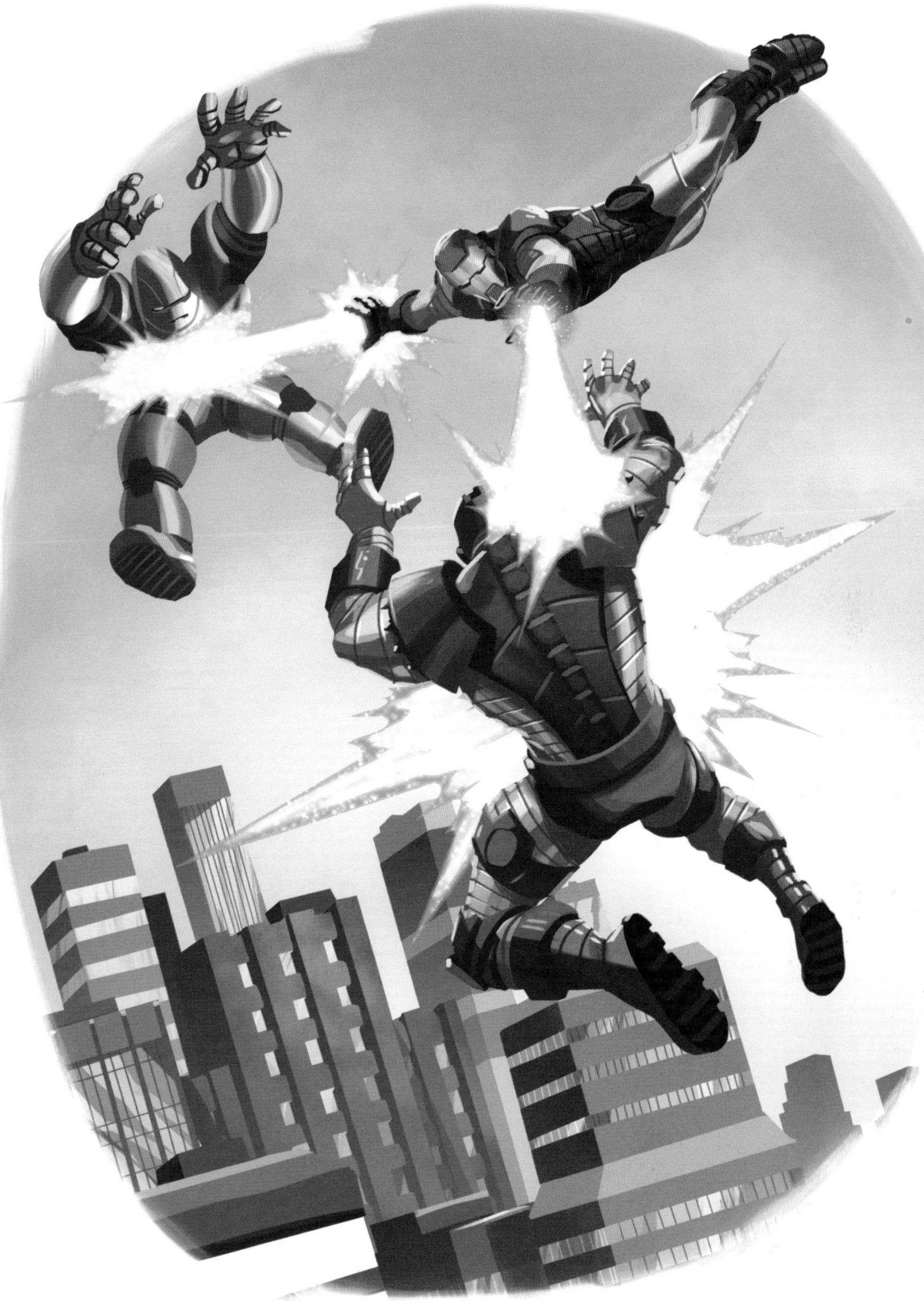

But with villains on the loose, such as Titanium Man and Iron Monger—who both use Tony's technology for their own evil purposes—

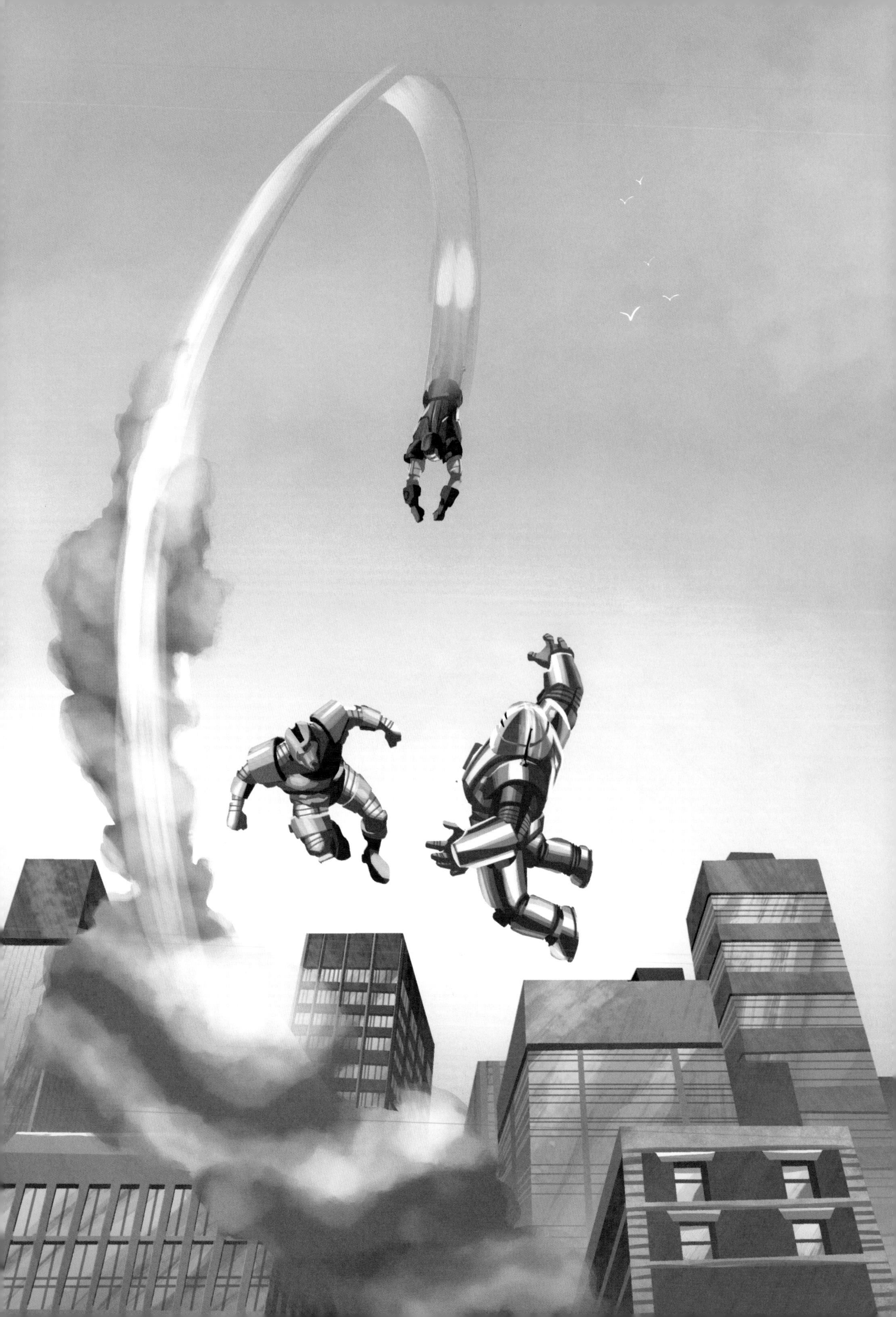

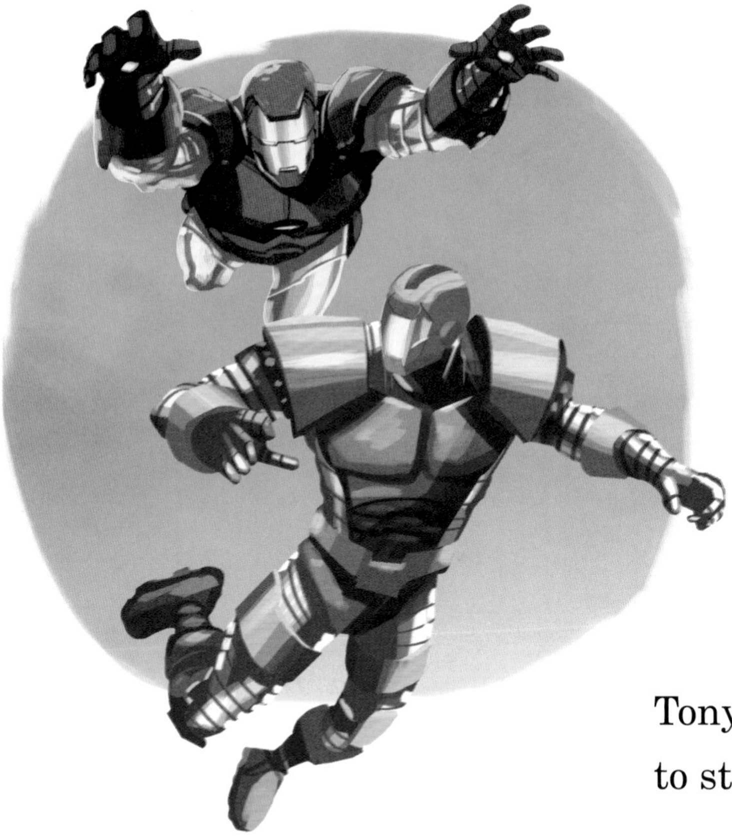

Tony feels it's his **responsibility** to stop them!

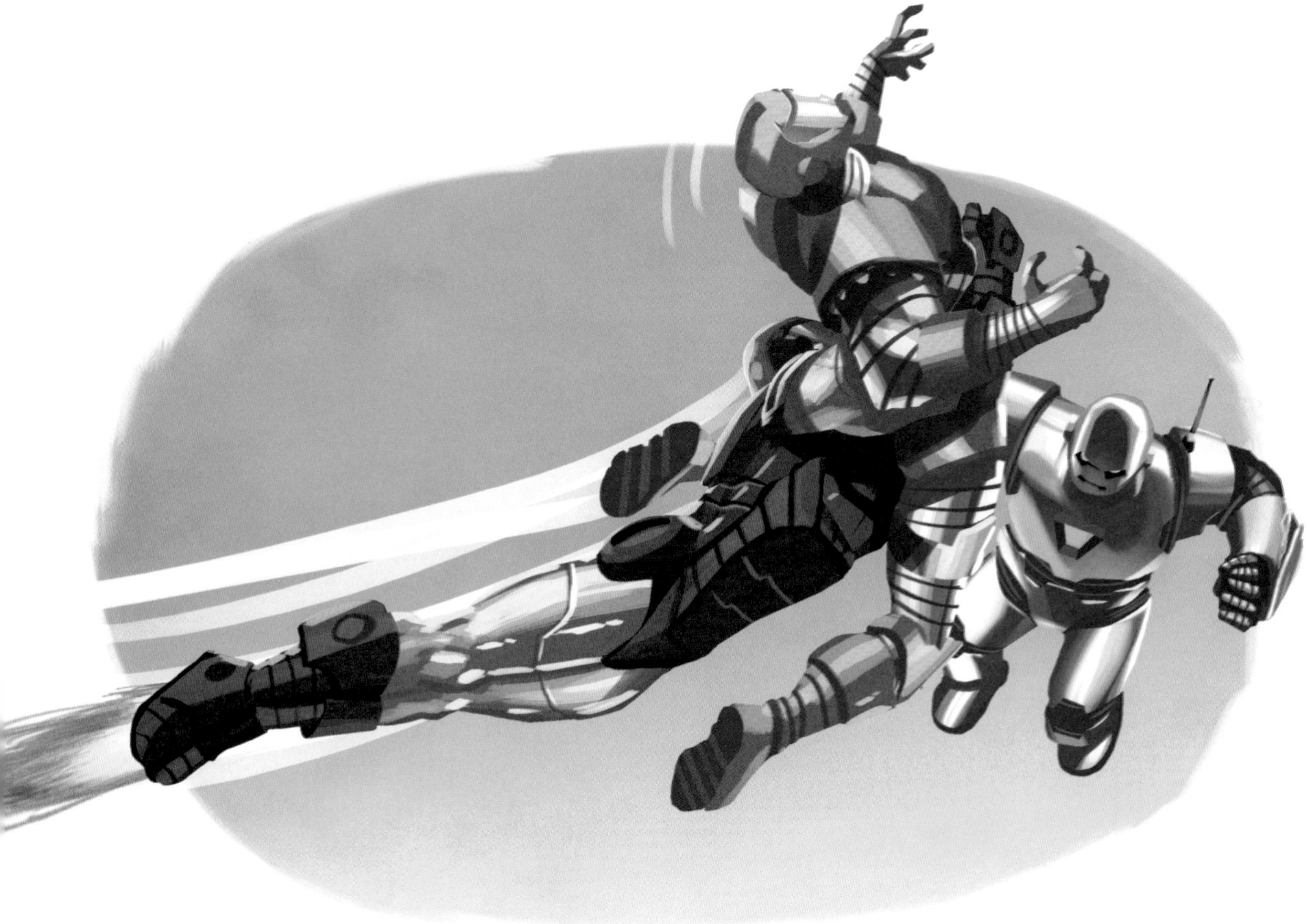

Tony didn't always get the job done this easily.

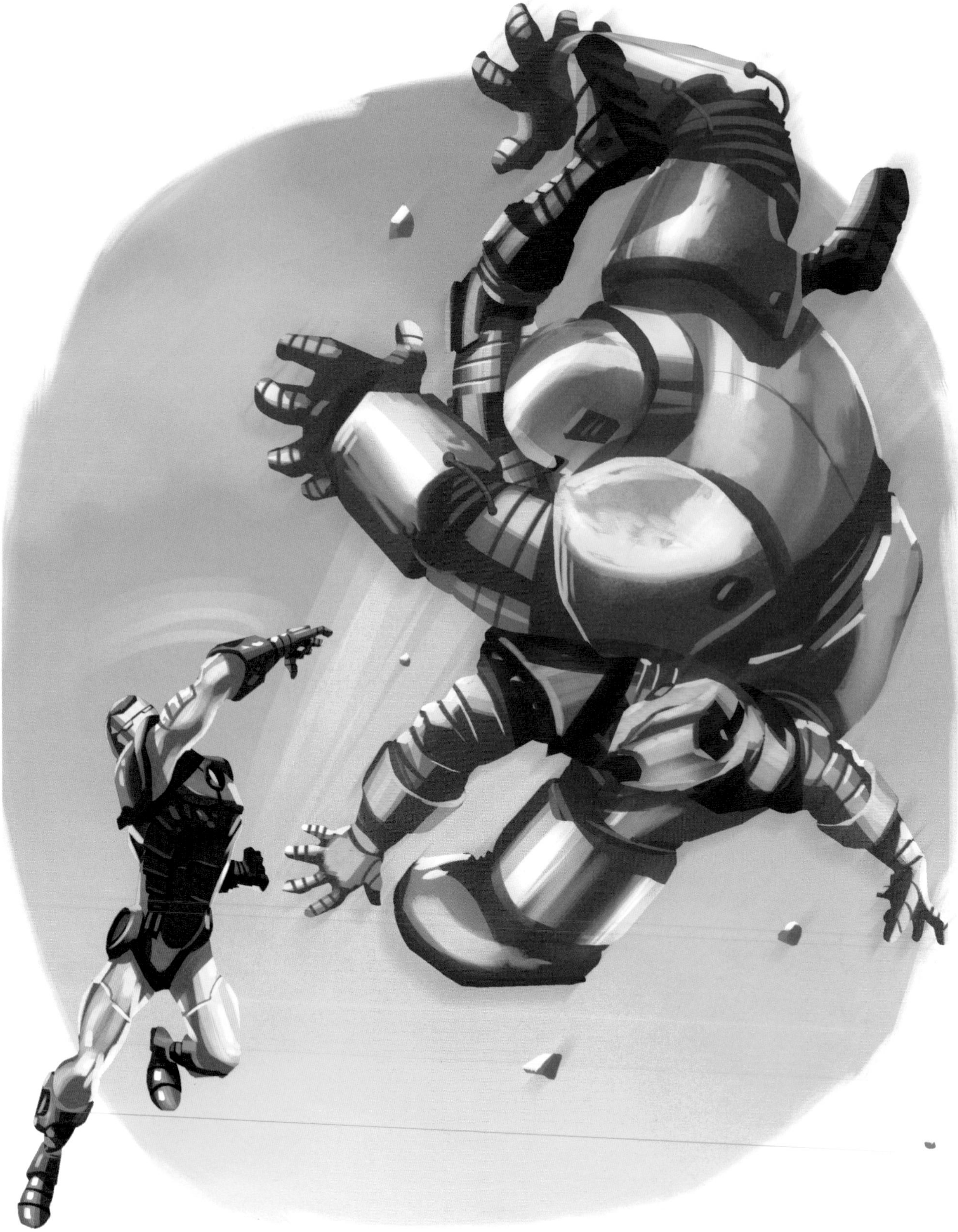

Or this well.

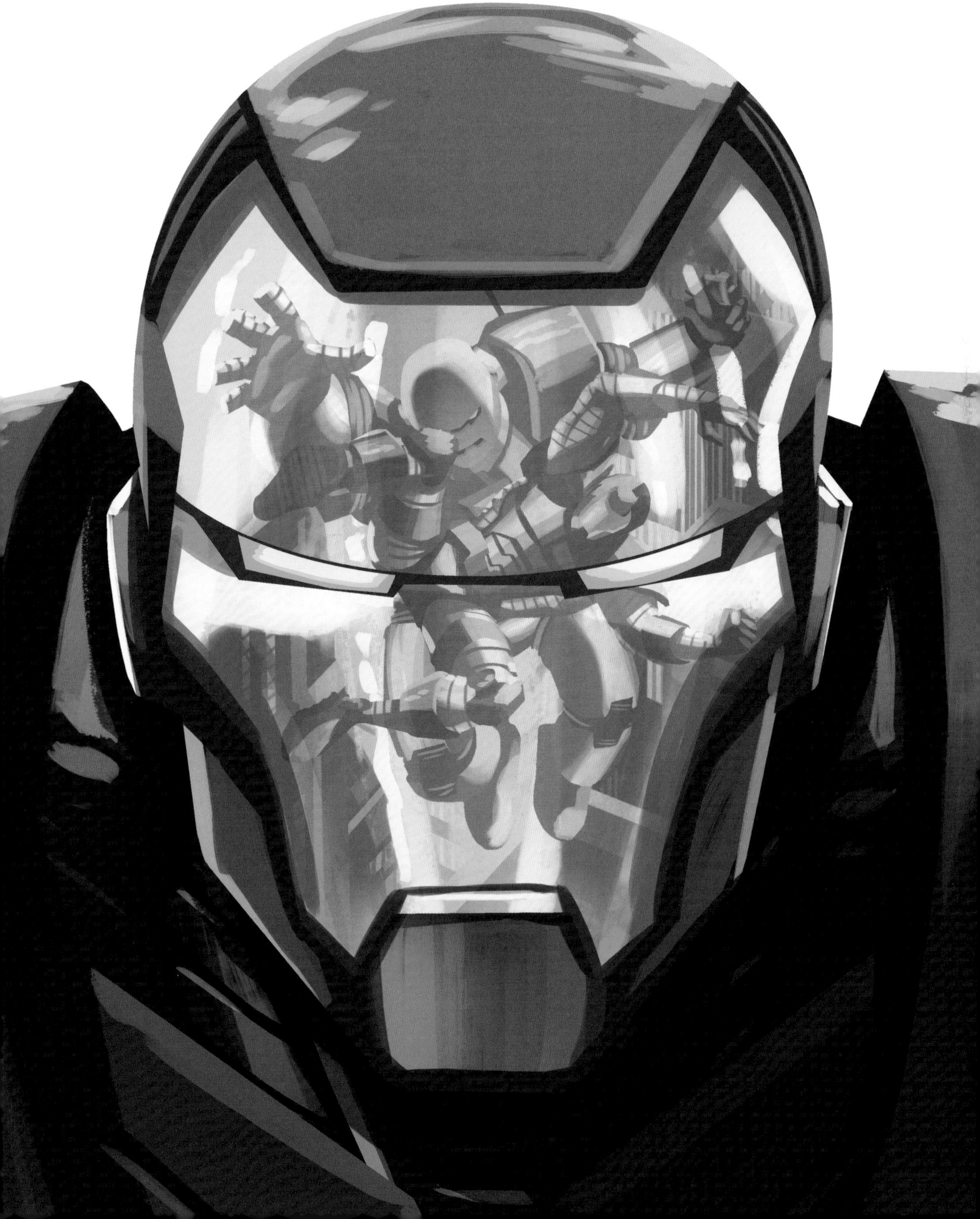

Tony's armor **wasn't always so sleek.**

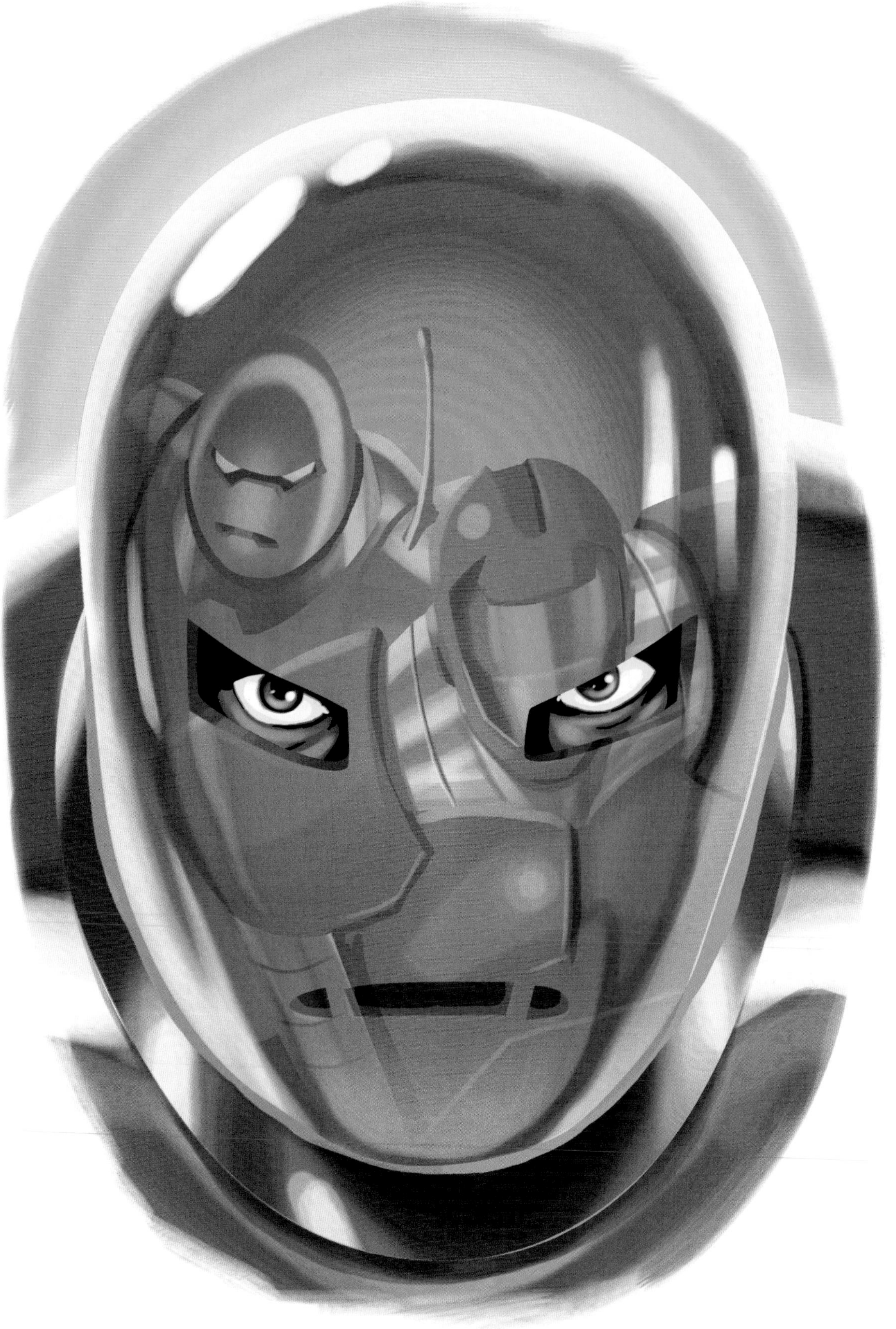

In fact, when he first became Iron Man, Tony's armor didn't even shine!

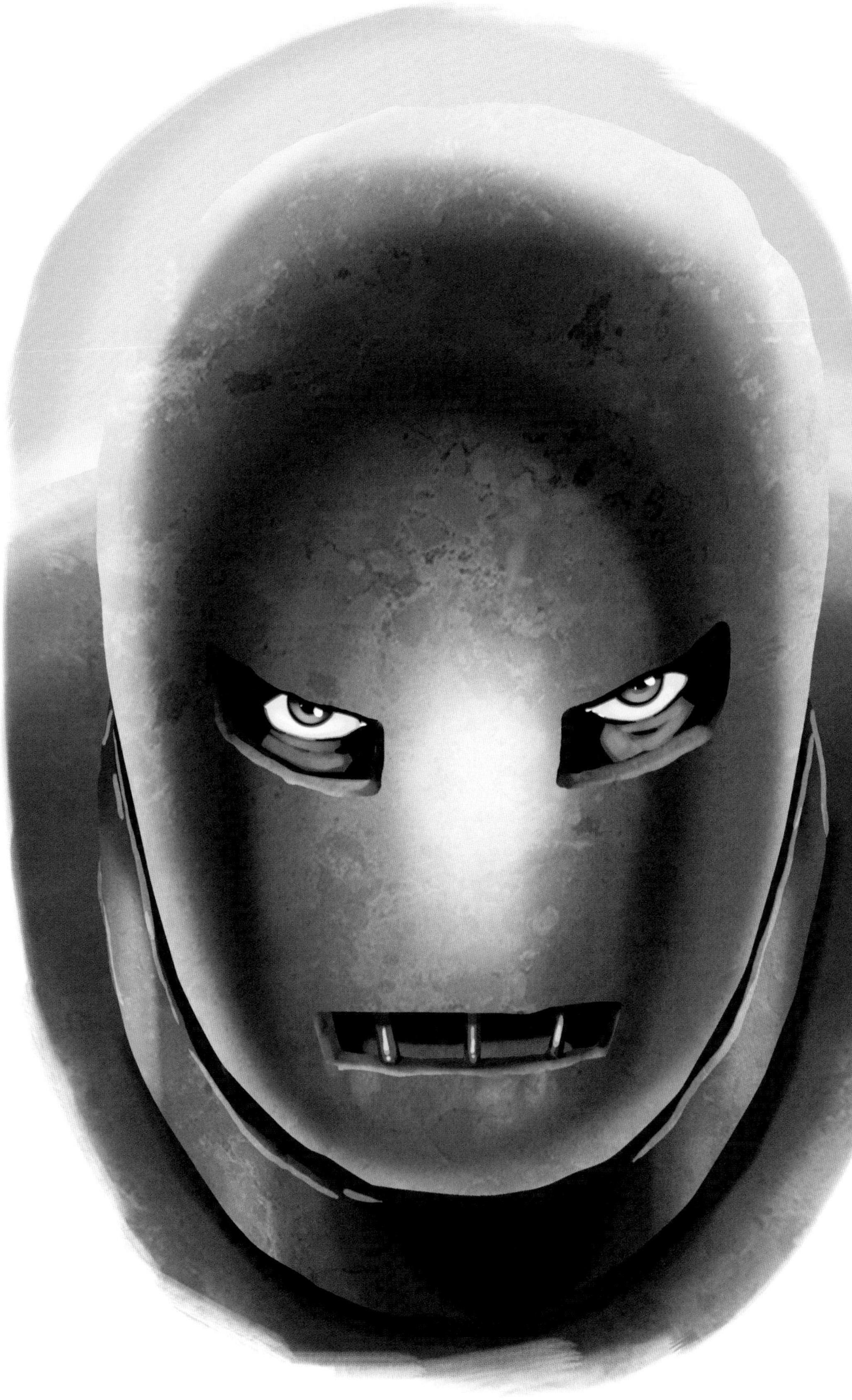

But if you really want to know how Iron Man was born, we need to start with the **man behind the mask.**
We need to start with TONY.

Tony had so much money that he could go anywhere he wanted.

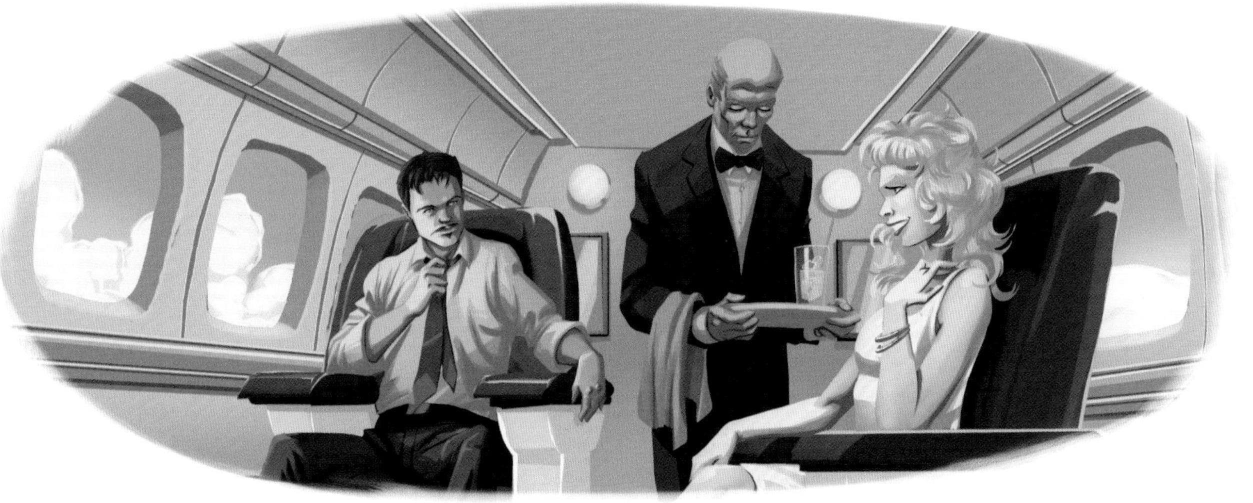

He loved to have fun.

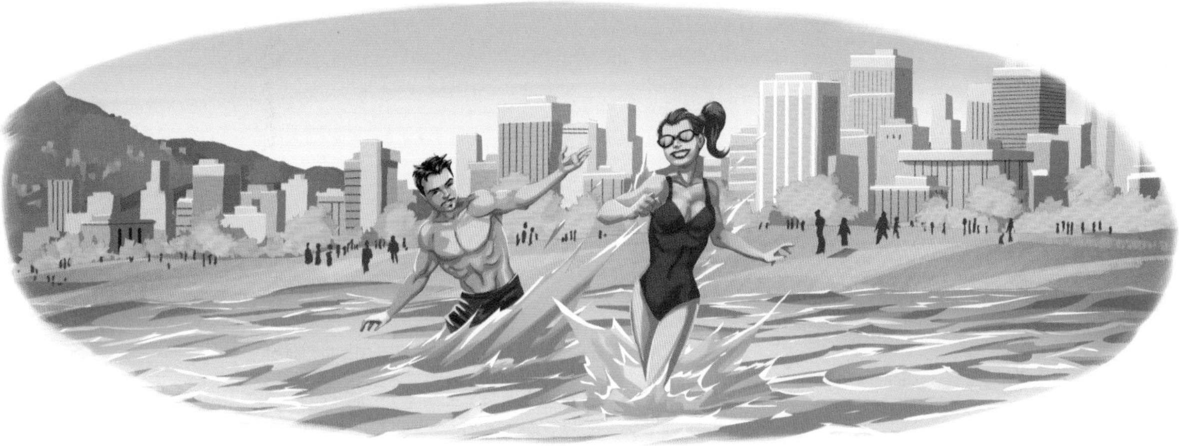

And he loved the finer things in life.

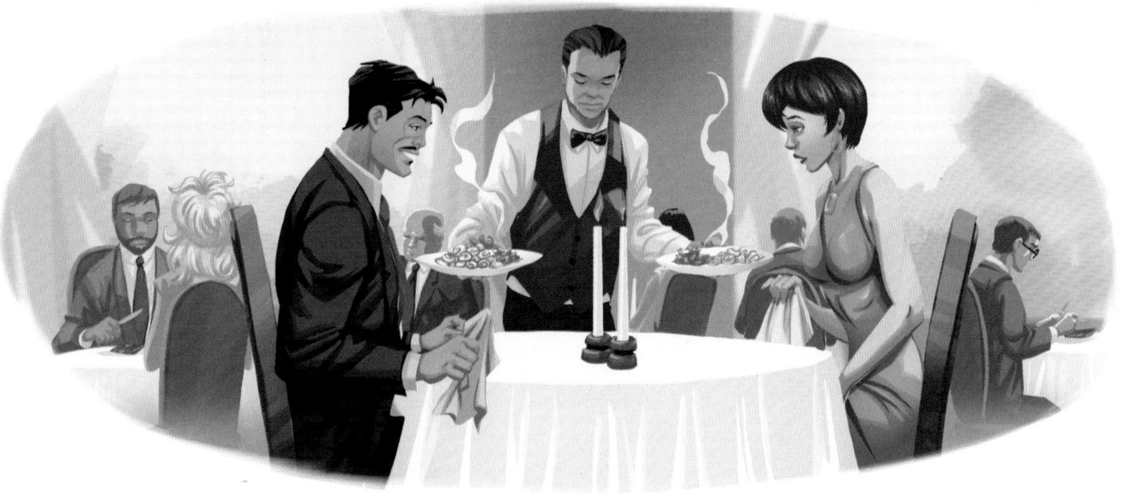

But Tony also worked hard.
He was a **brilliant inventor.**
He knew all sorts of things
about **science.**

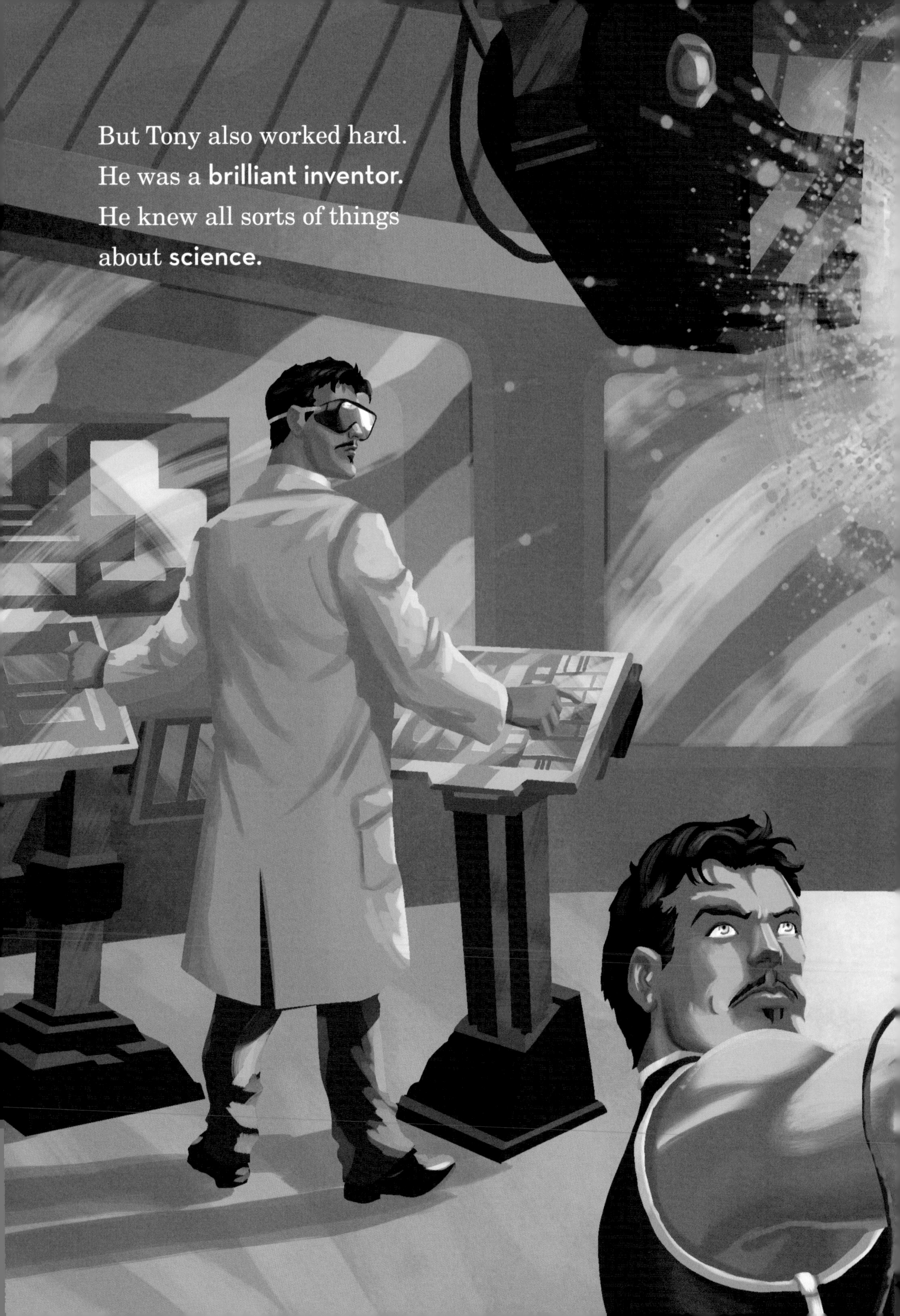

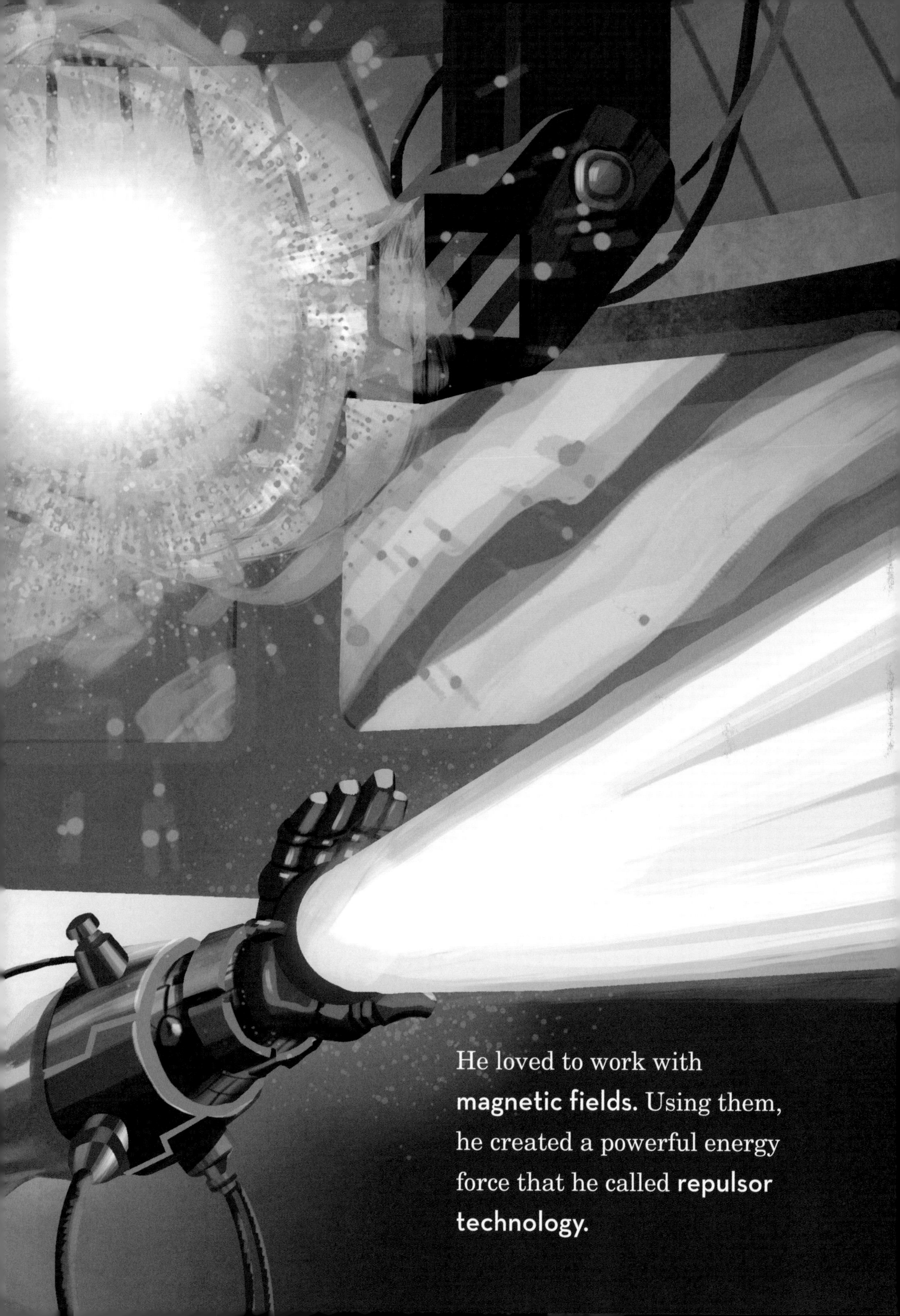

He loved to work with **magnetic fields.** Using them, he created a powerful energy force that he called **repulsor technology.**

The military was interested in Tony's work. In fact, it was in a secret Army lab that Tony's life was forever changed.

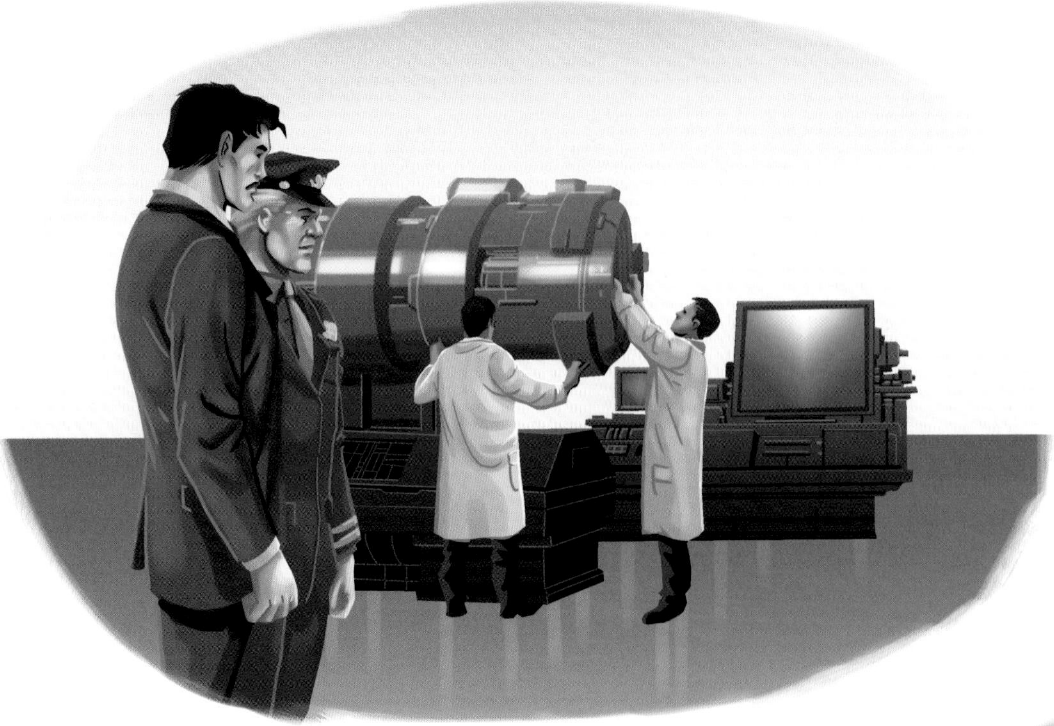

An enemy army had attacked, and Tony was badly hurt!

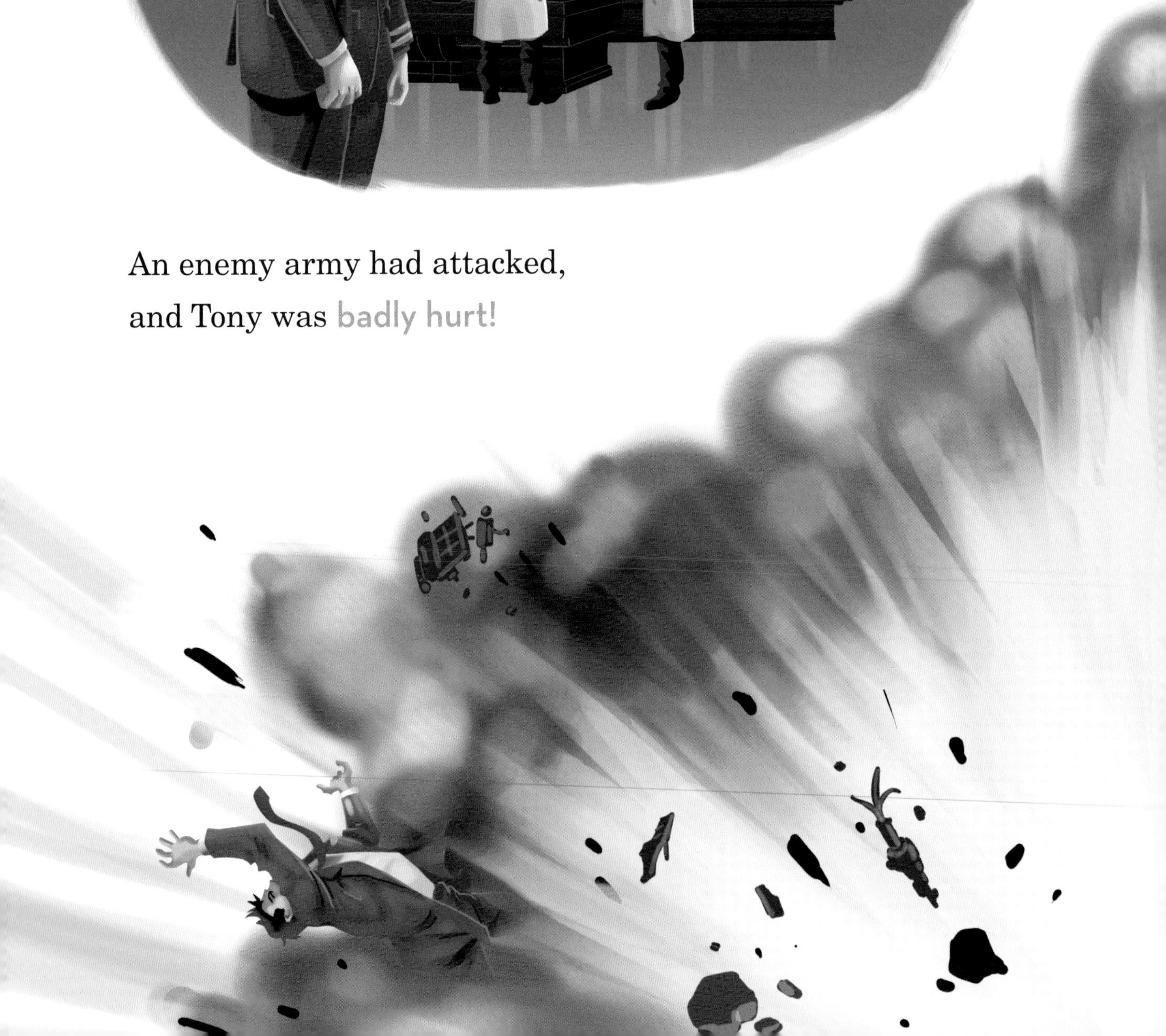

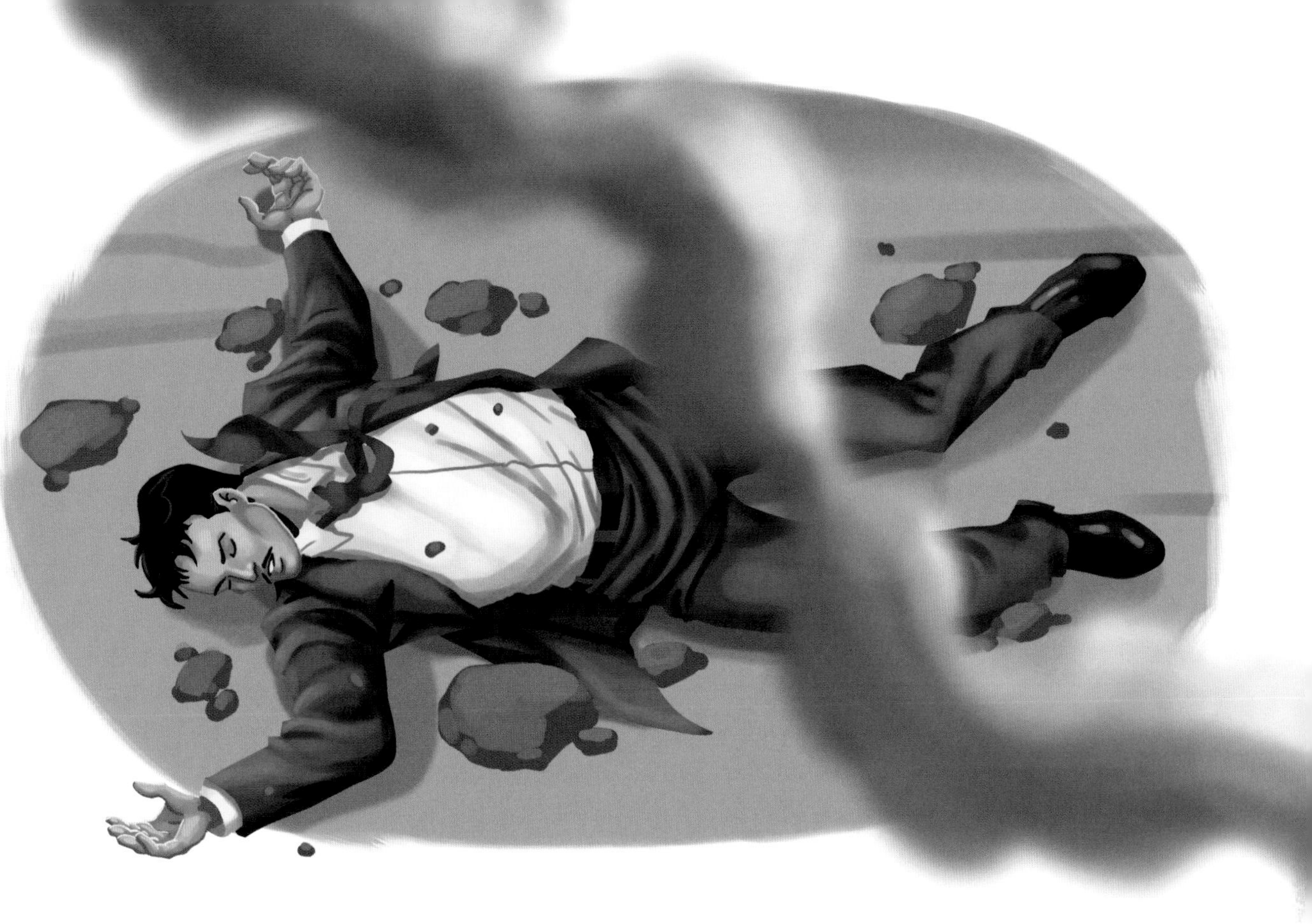

Since Tony was famous, he was recognized right away.
The enemy knew all about his inventions.

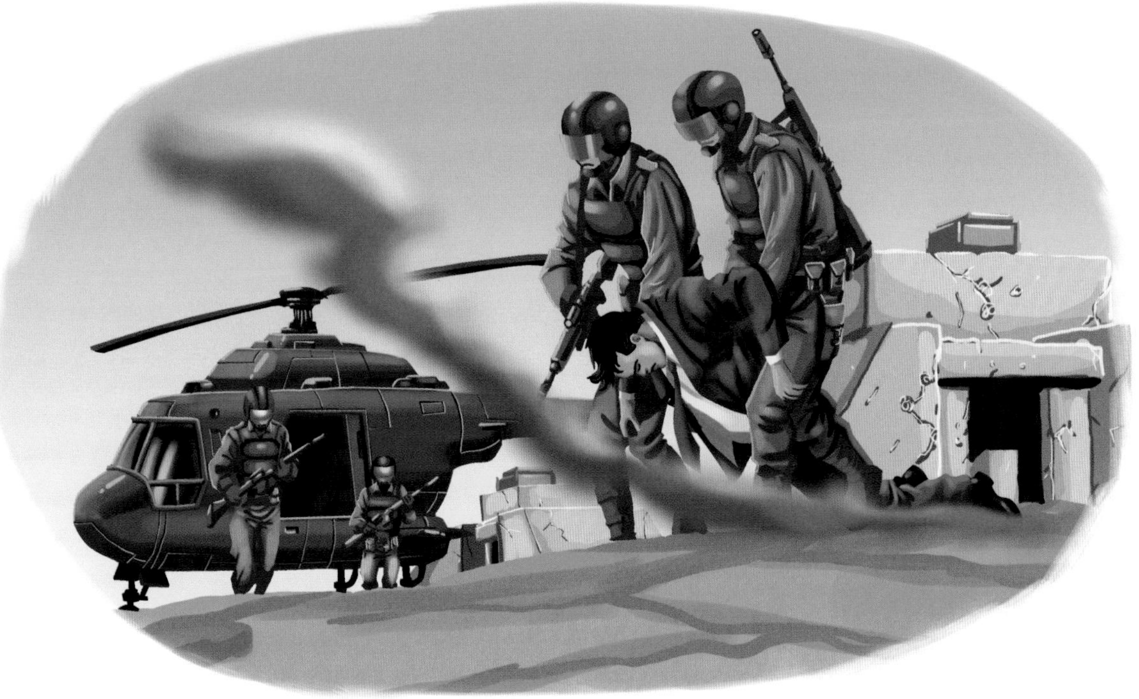

They tossed him in a prison room filled with electronic and mechanical equipment. They wanted him to create a mighty weapon for them.

To make things worse, before the enemy left the tiny cell, they told Tony that his heart had been hurt in the blast. He did not have much longer to live.

Tony soon found he was not alone in the cell. The enemy had captured another famous scientist—**PROFESSOR YINSEN.** The enemy wanted the two men to work together on the great weapon.

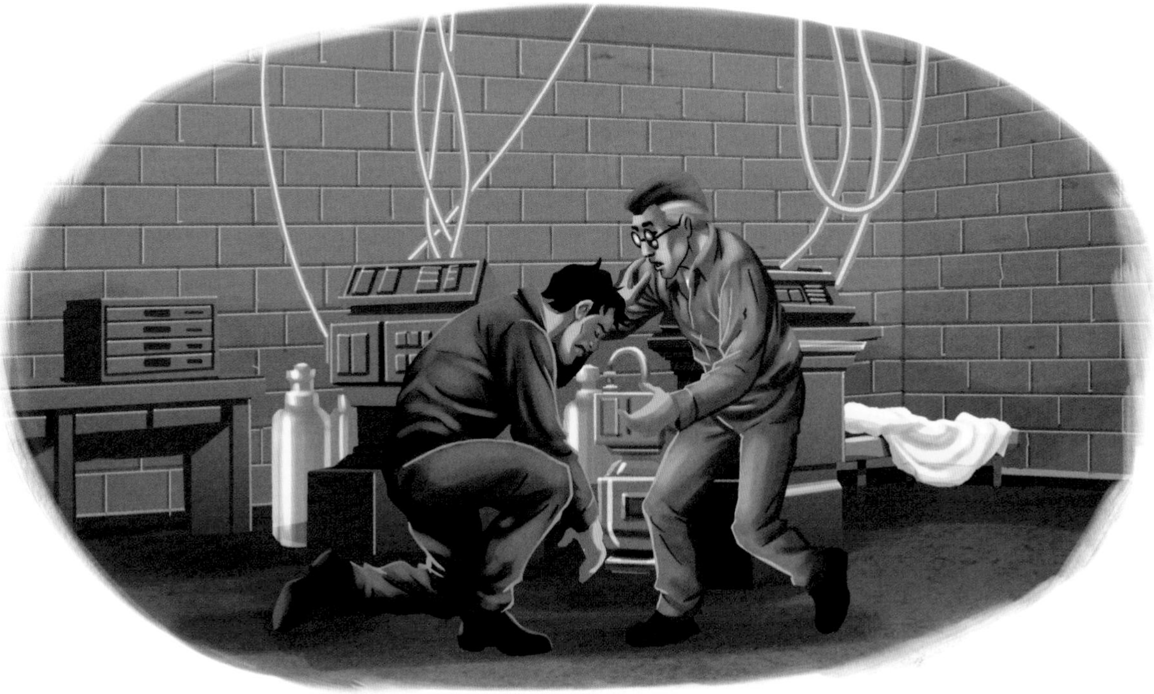

But Professor Yinsen had other ideas—he knew a way to keep Tony alive!

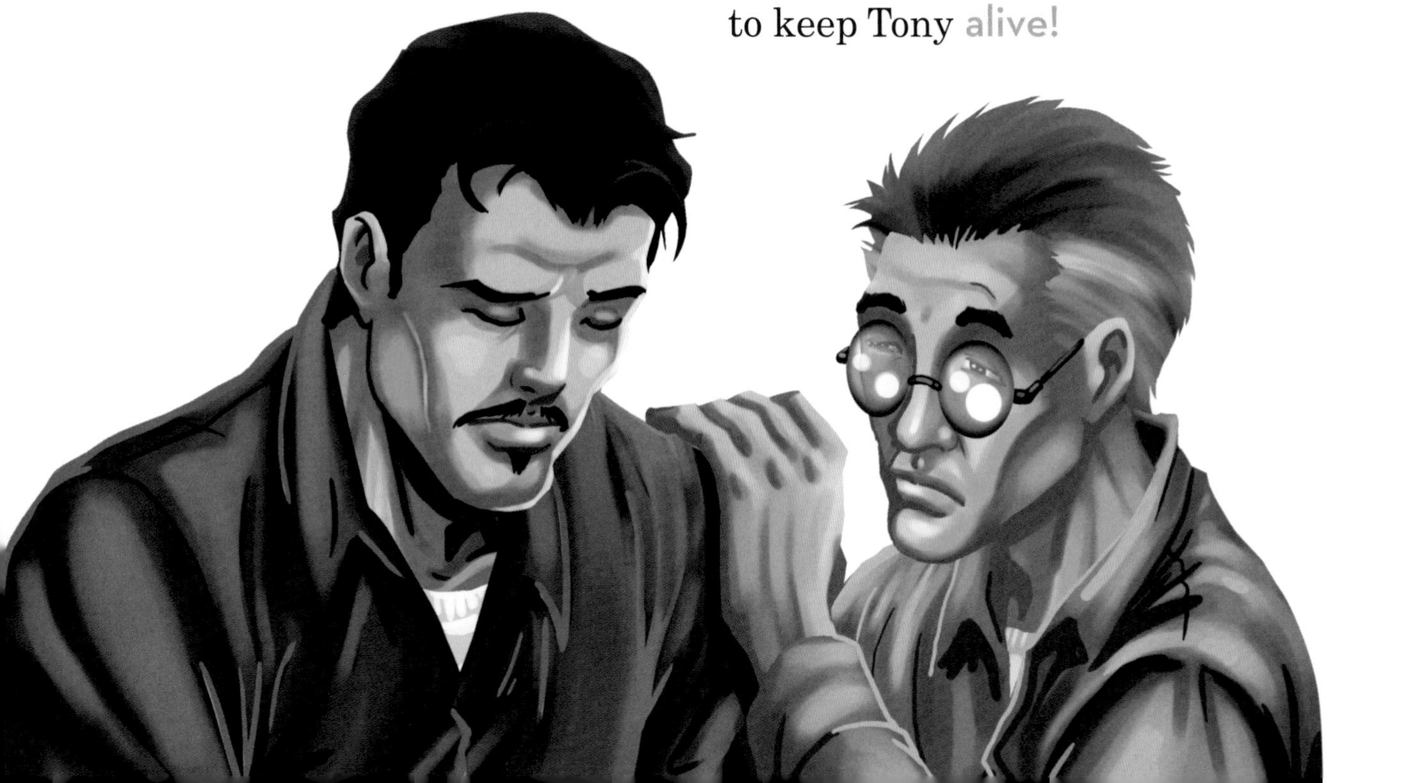

The two men **worked tirelessly** to create something that would save Tony's life . . .

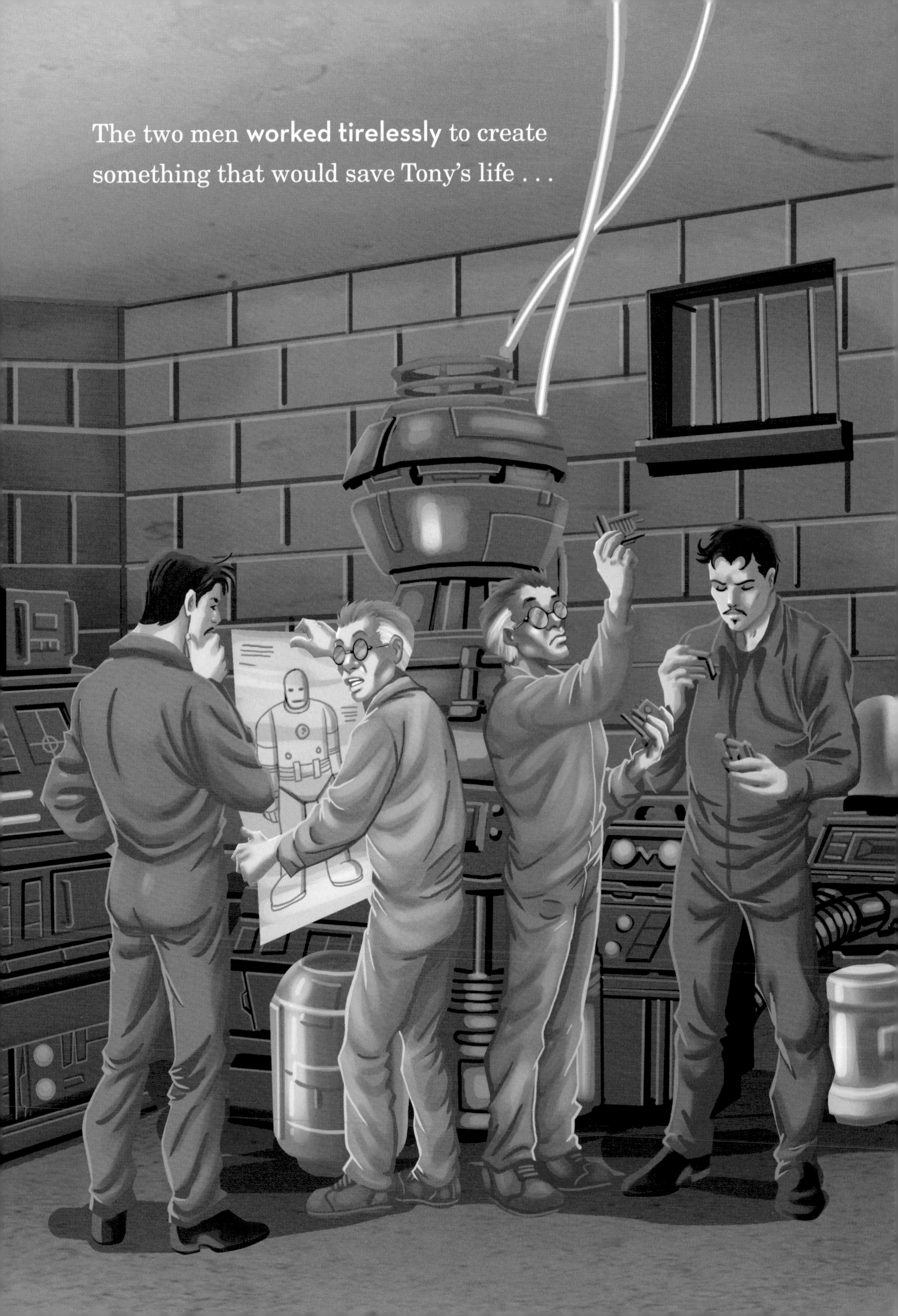

. . . and at the same time, help them to **escape** the prison!

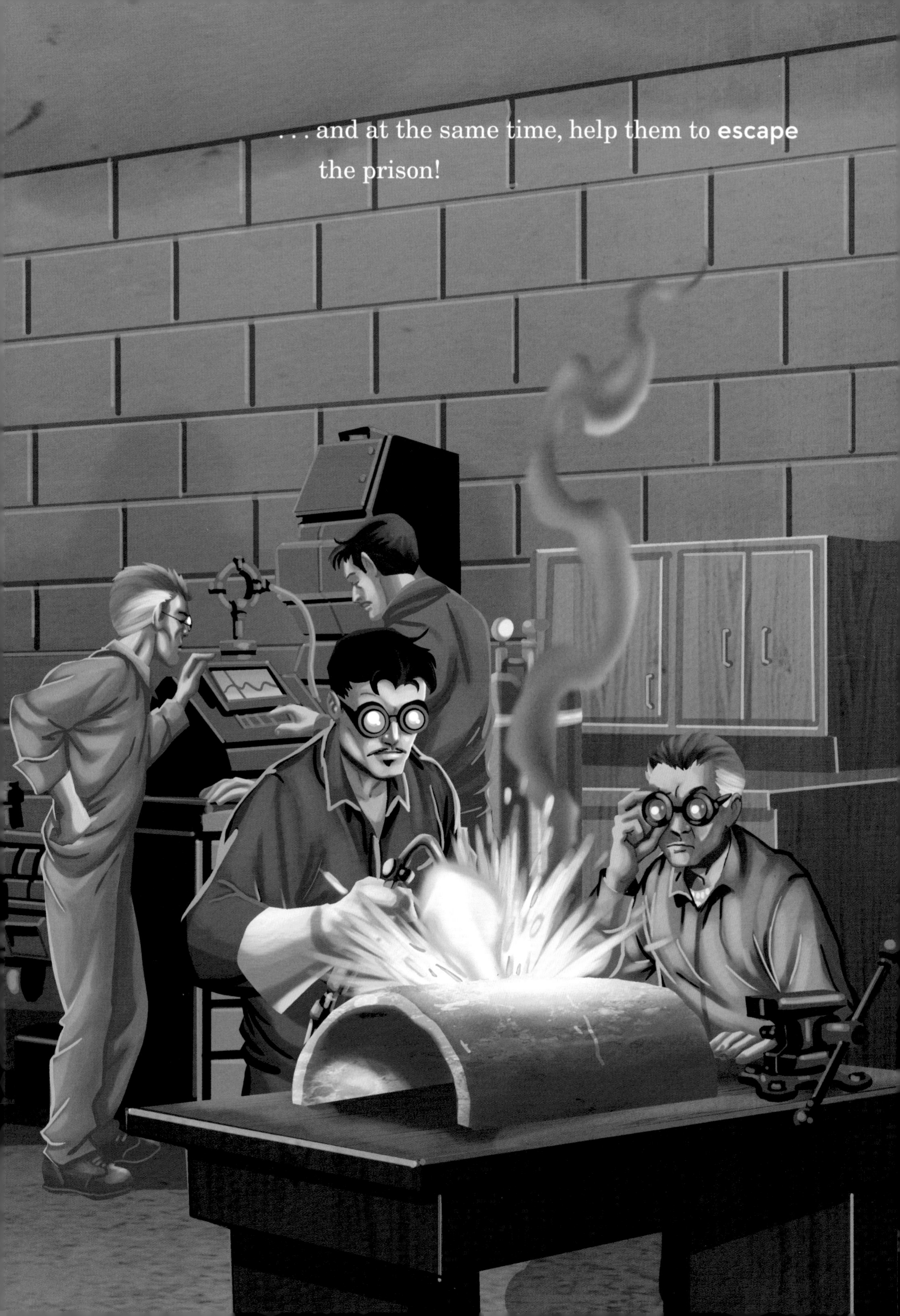

Finally, the men completed the device that from now on Tony would always need to wear on his chest to keep his heart beating.

But that wasn't all they had created.

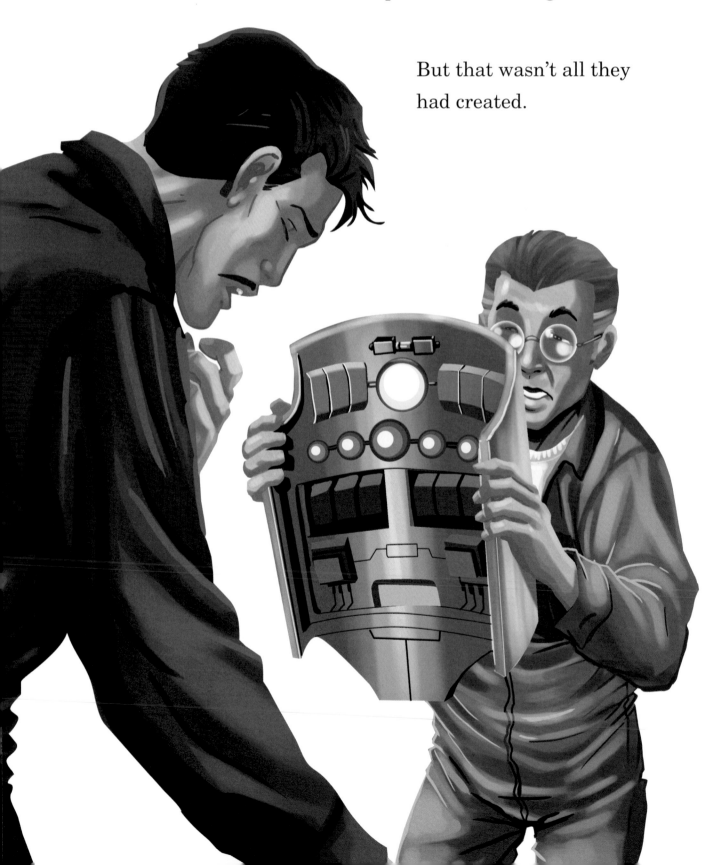

Using Tony's repulsors, they had built boots that could help a man fly!

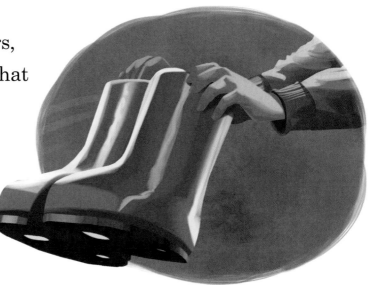

Gloves that could crush steel!

And a helmet that could protect a man from the most terrible blast!

Tony put on the armor...

. . . and proved that no walls could hold

the IRON MAN!

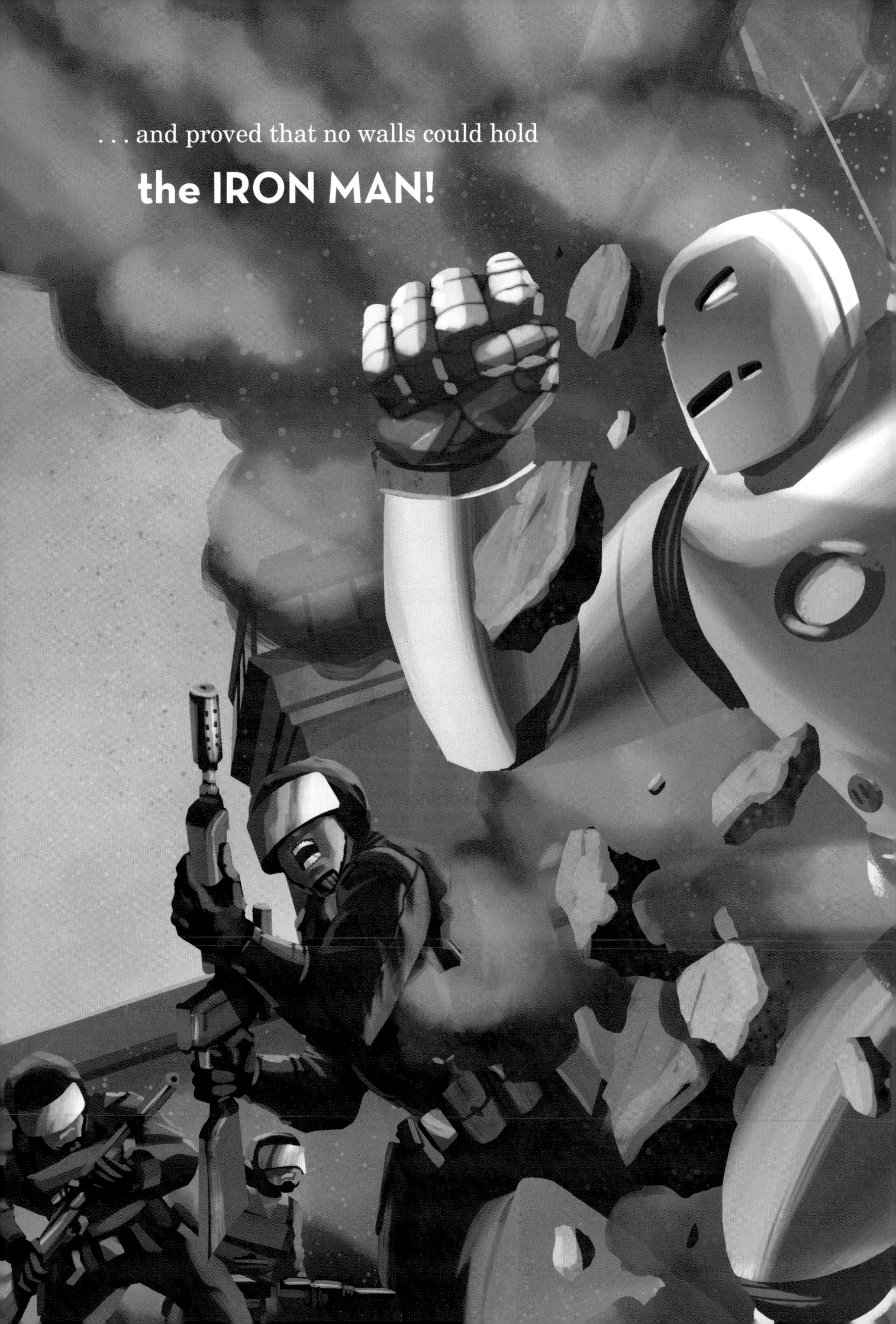

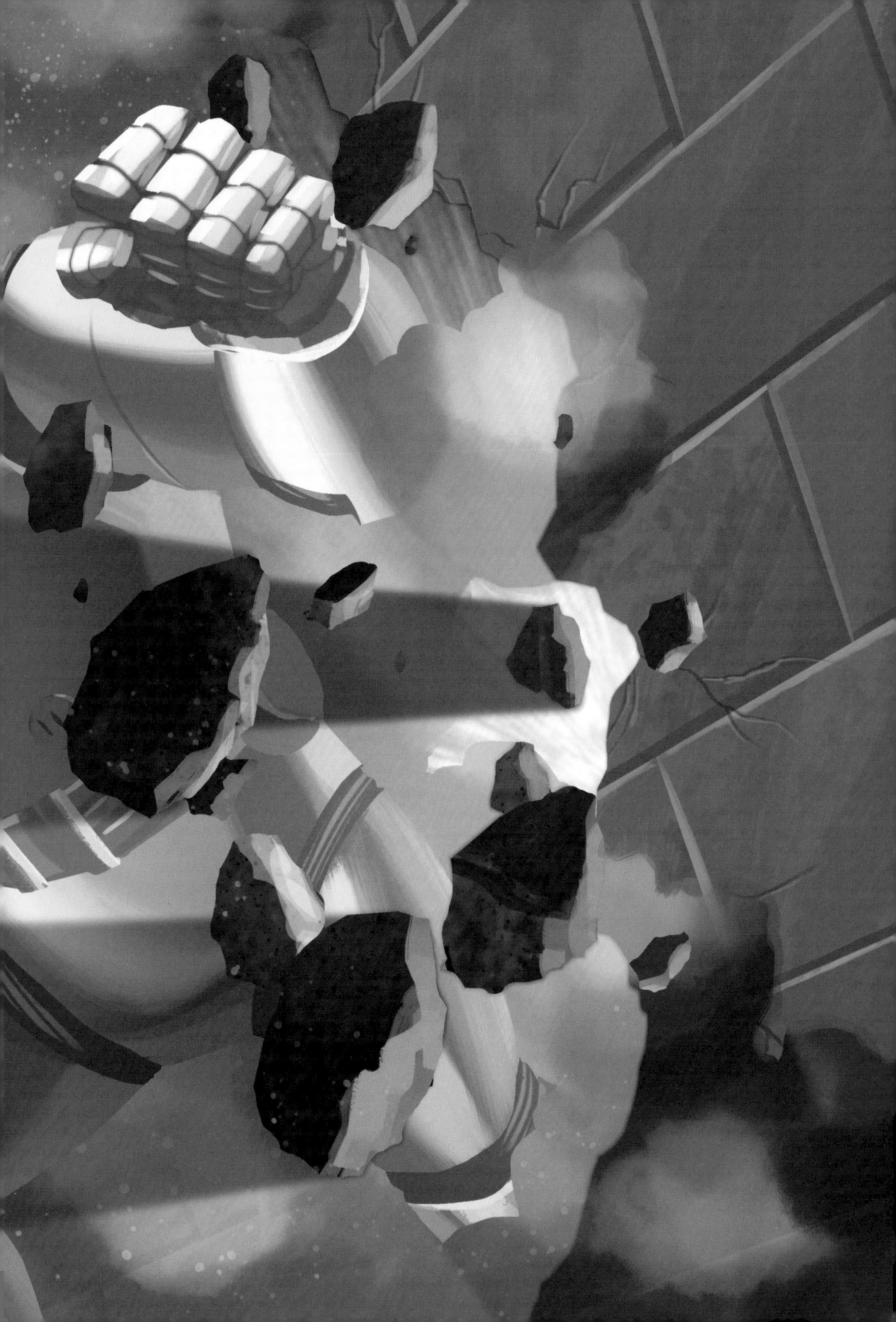

It wasn't long before
the enemy realized . . .

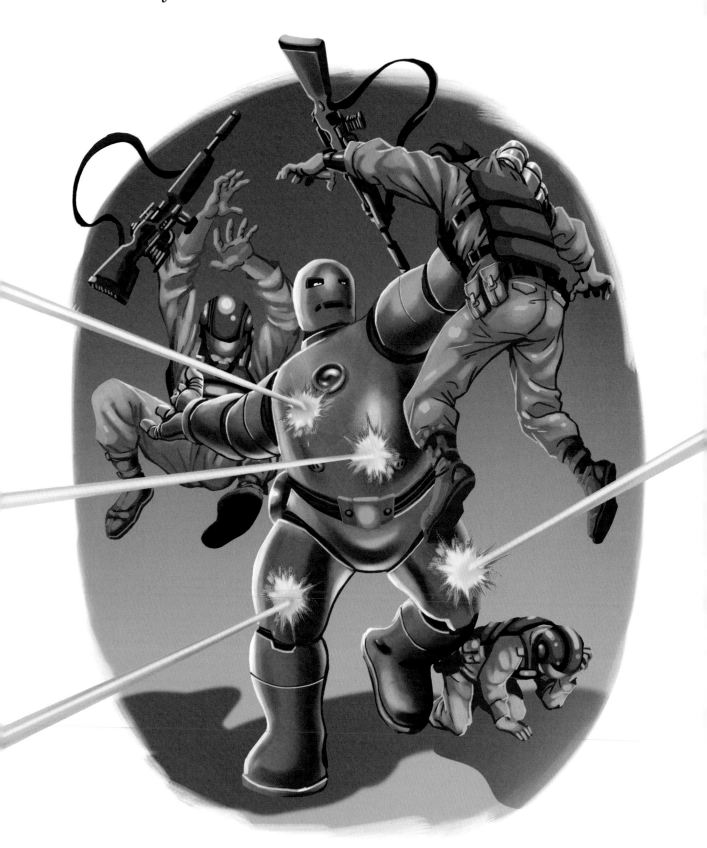

. . . they were fighting a losing battle.

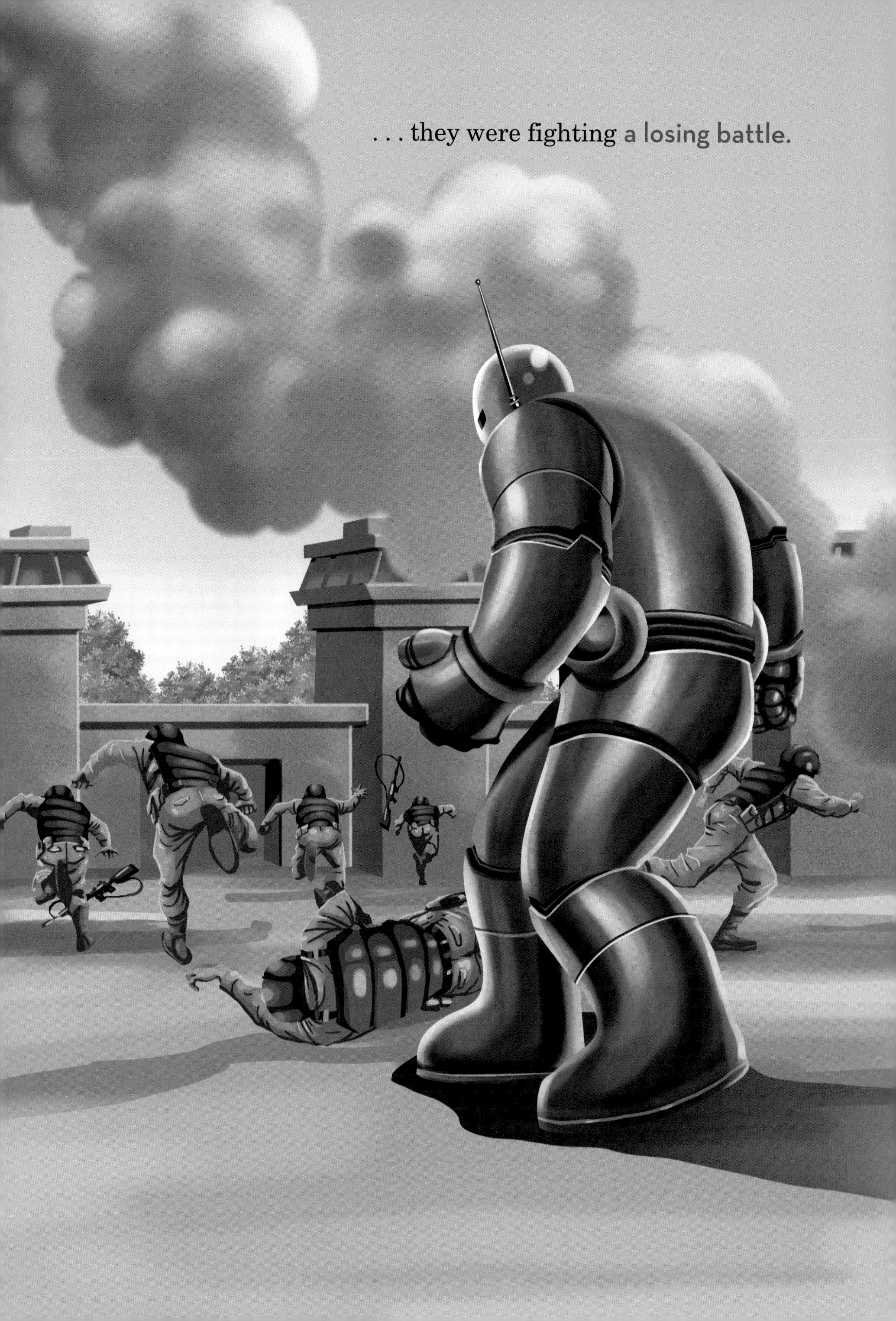

Having escaped from prison and saved Professor Yinsen, Tony flew back home.

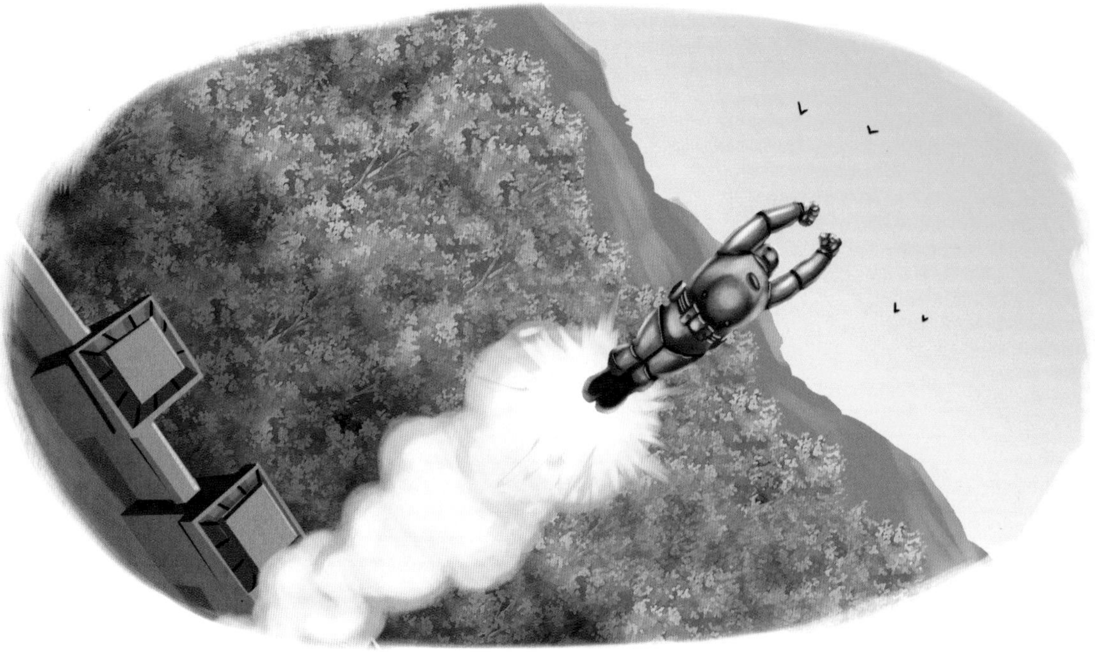

But almost as soon as he got there, he realized that he could now help where others couldn't.

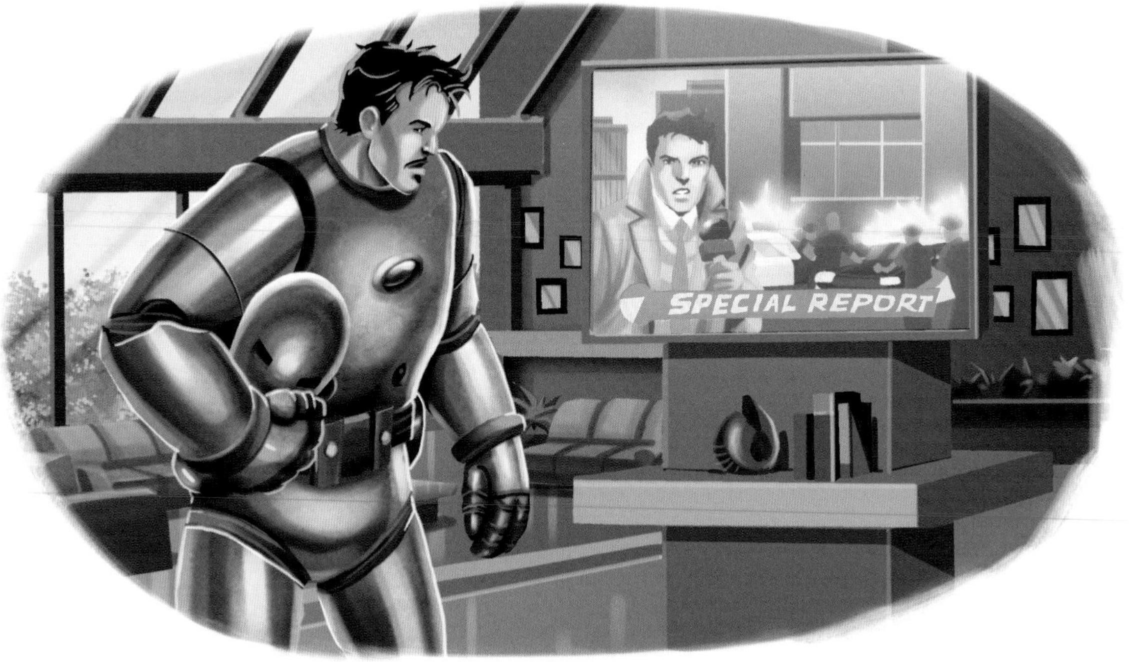
SPECIAL REPORT

Tony to the rescue!

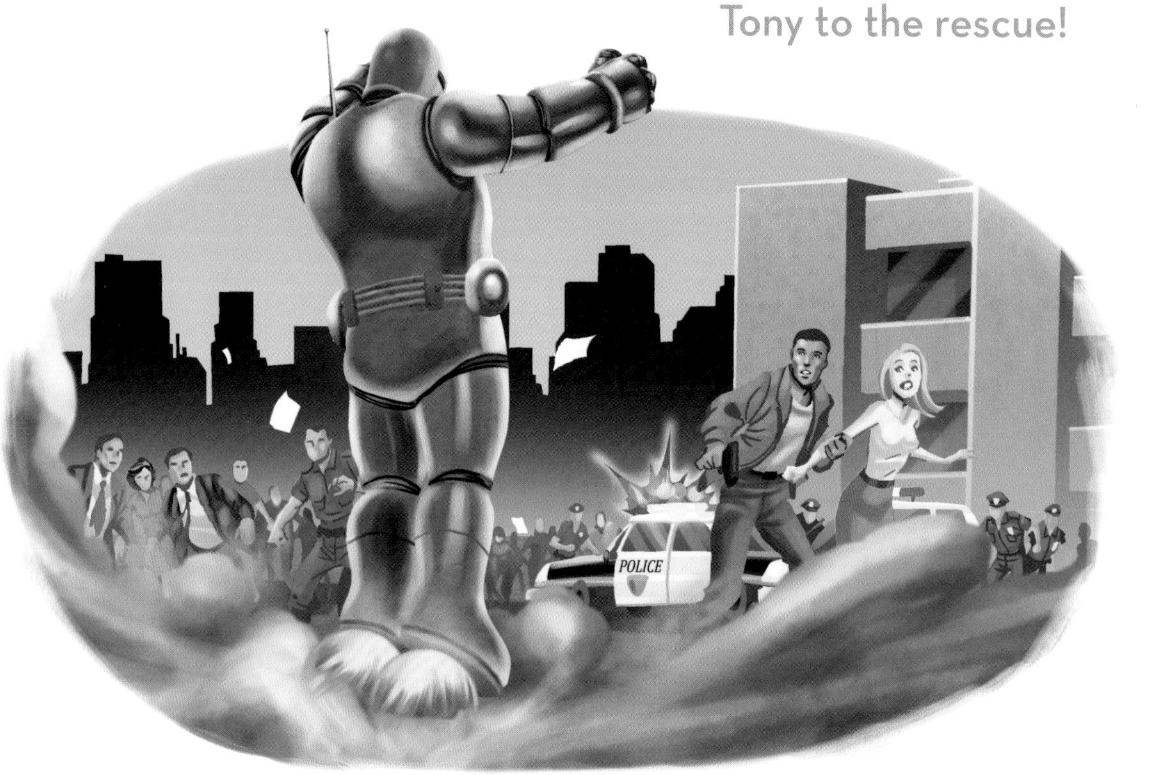
POLICE

He was strong, unstoppable, **FRIGHTENING!**

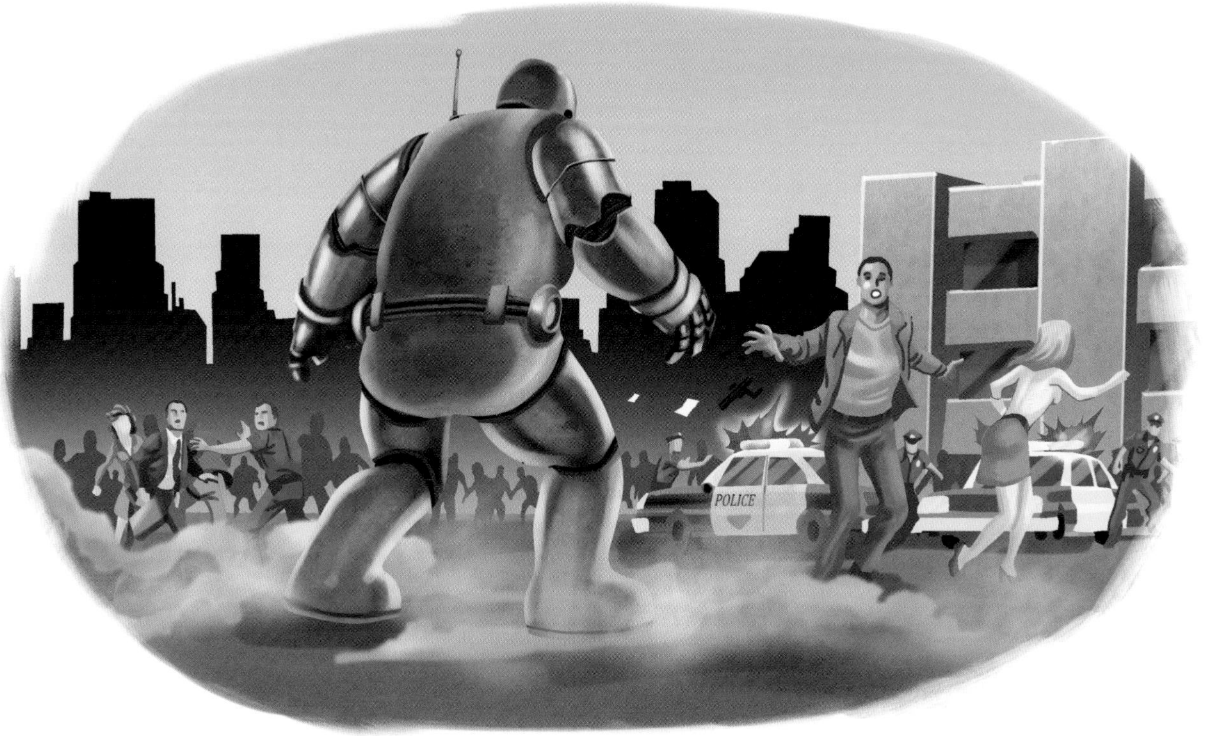
POLICE

Maybe a little **too frightening.**

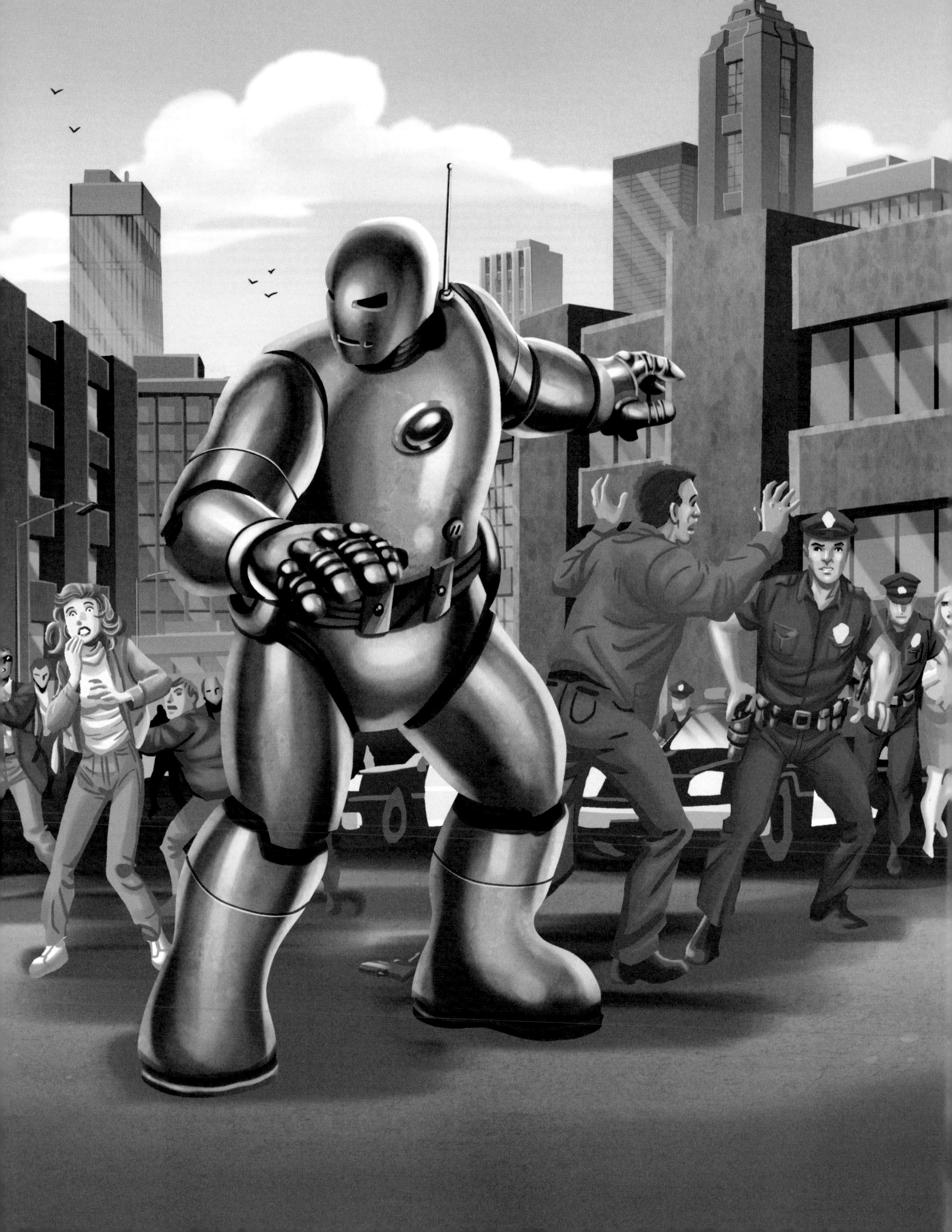

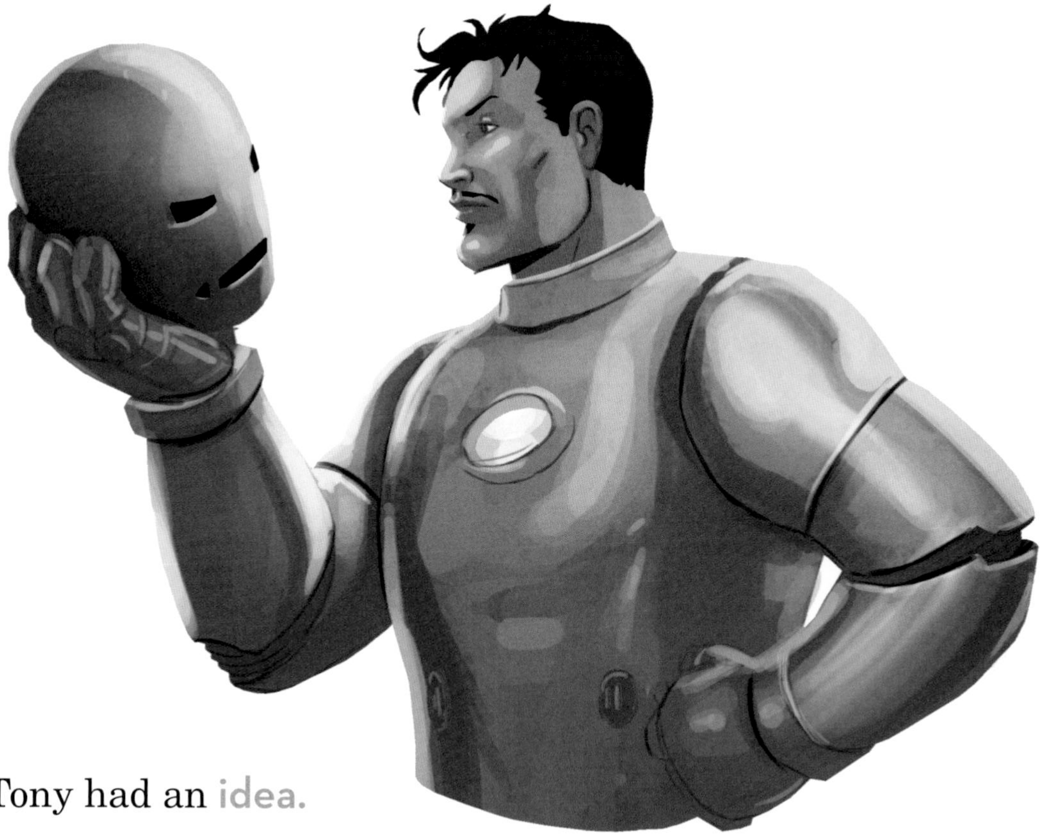

Tony had an idea.

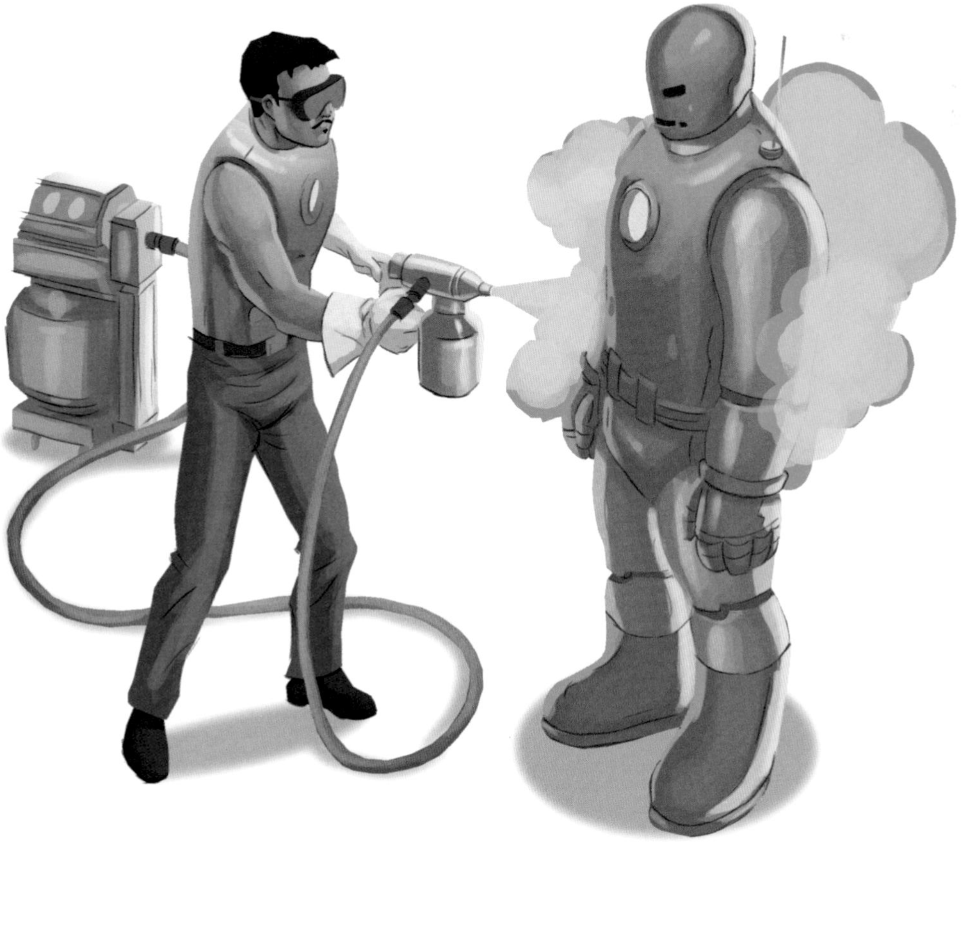

There.

That was better.

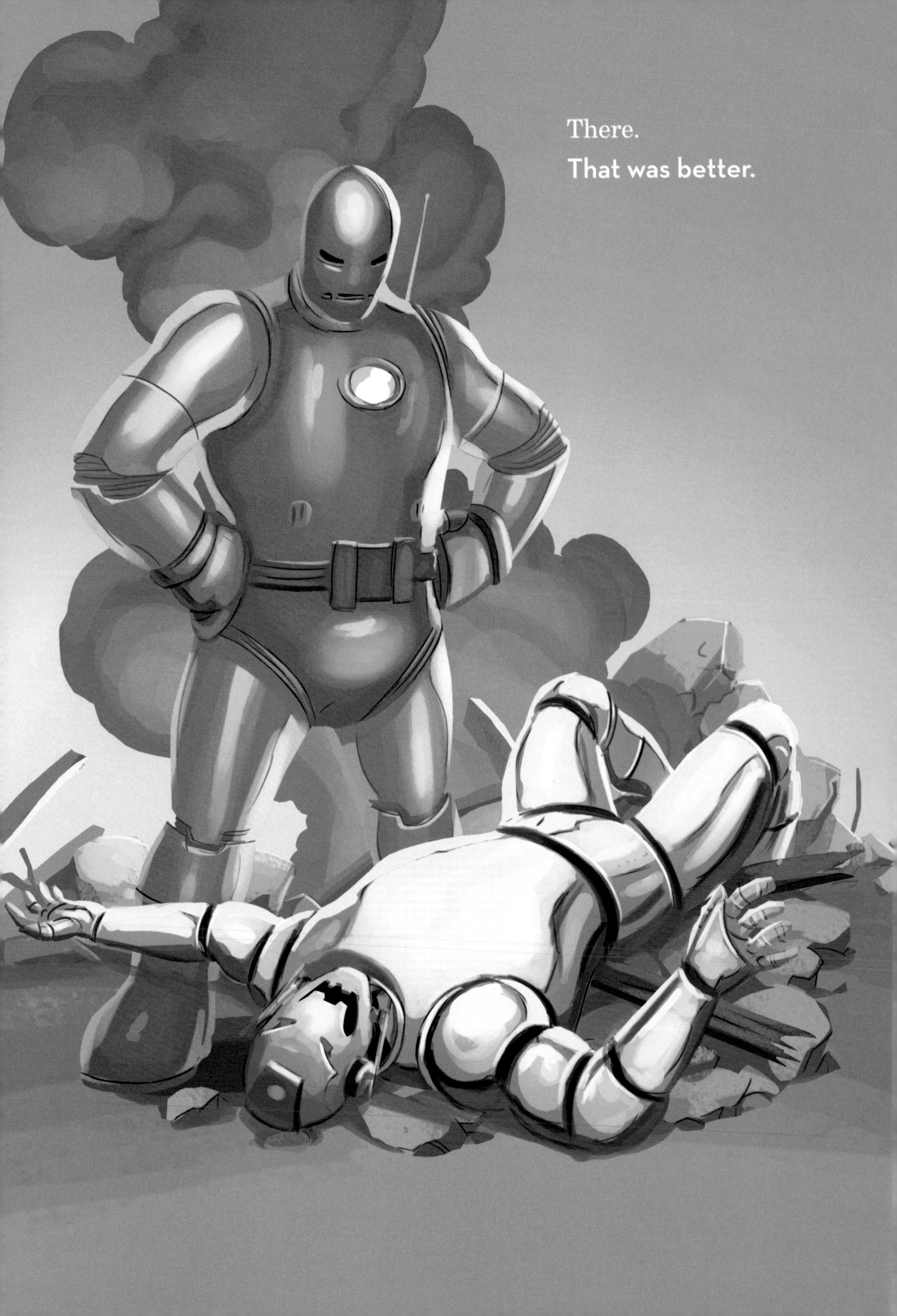

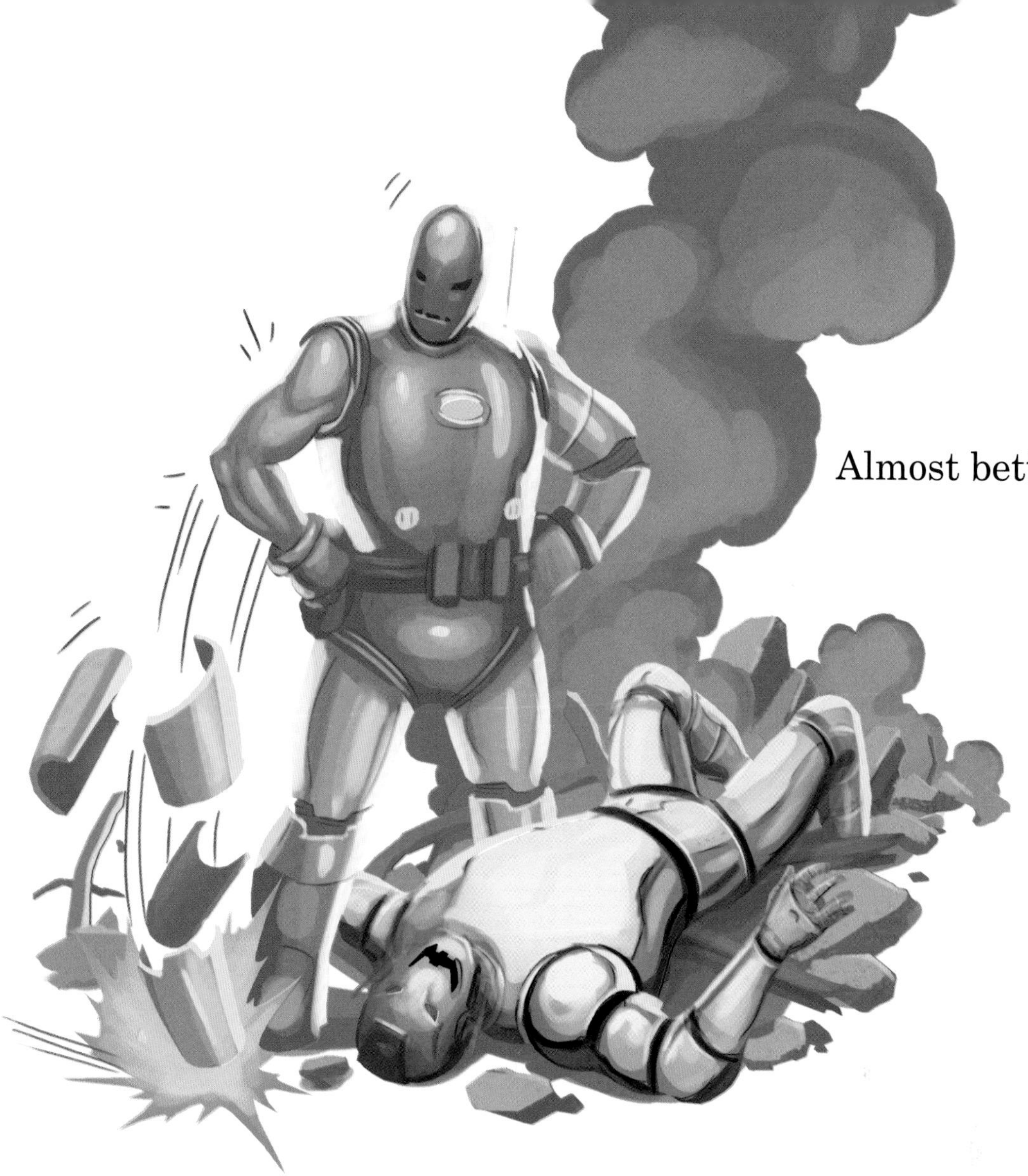

Almost better.

Back to the drawing board.

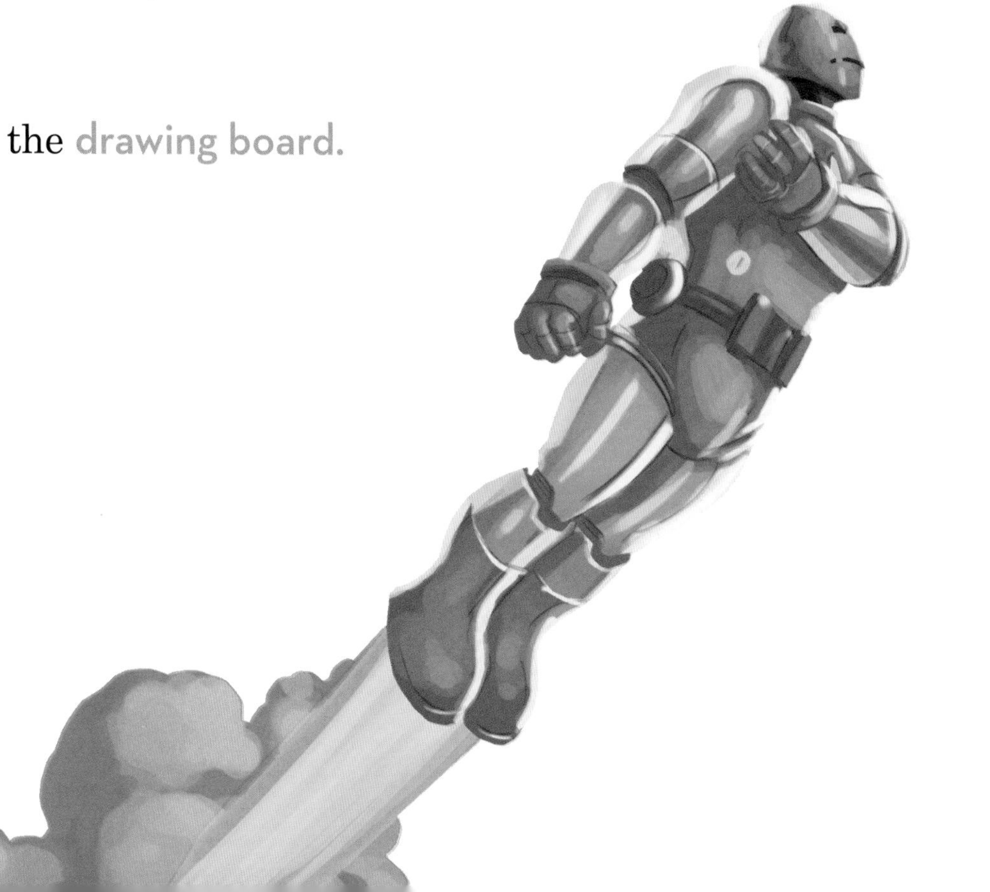

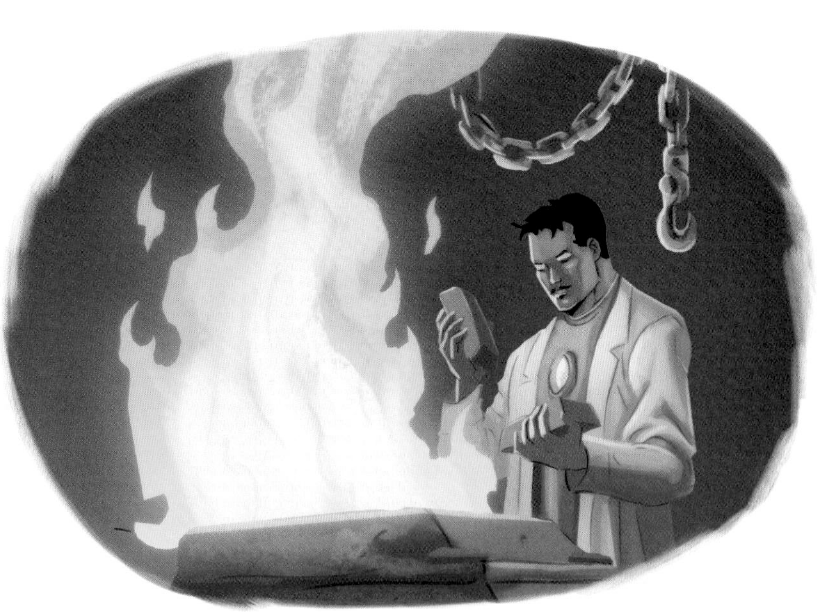

Tony thought that Iron Man needed something as smooth and stylish as he was.

He needed to create a lighter suit.

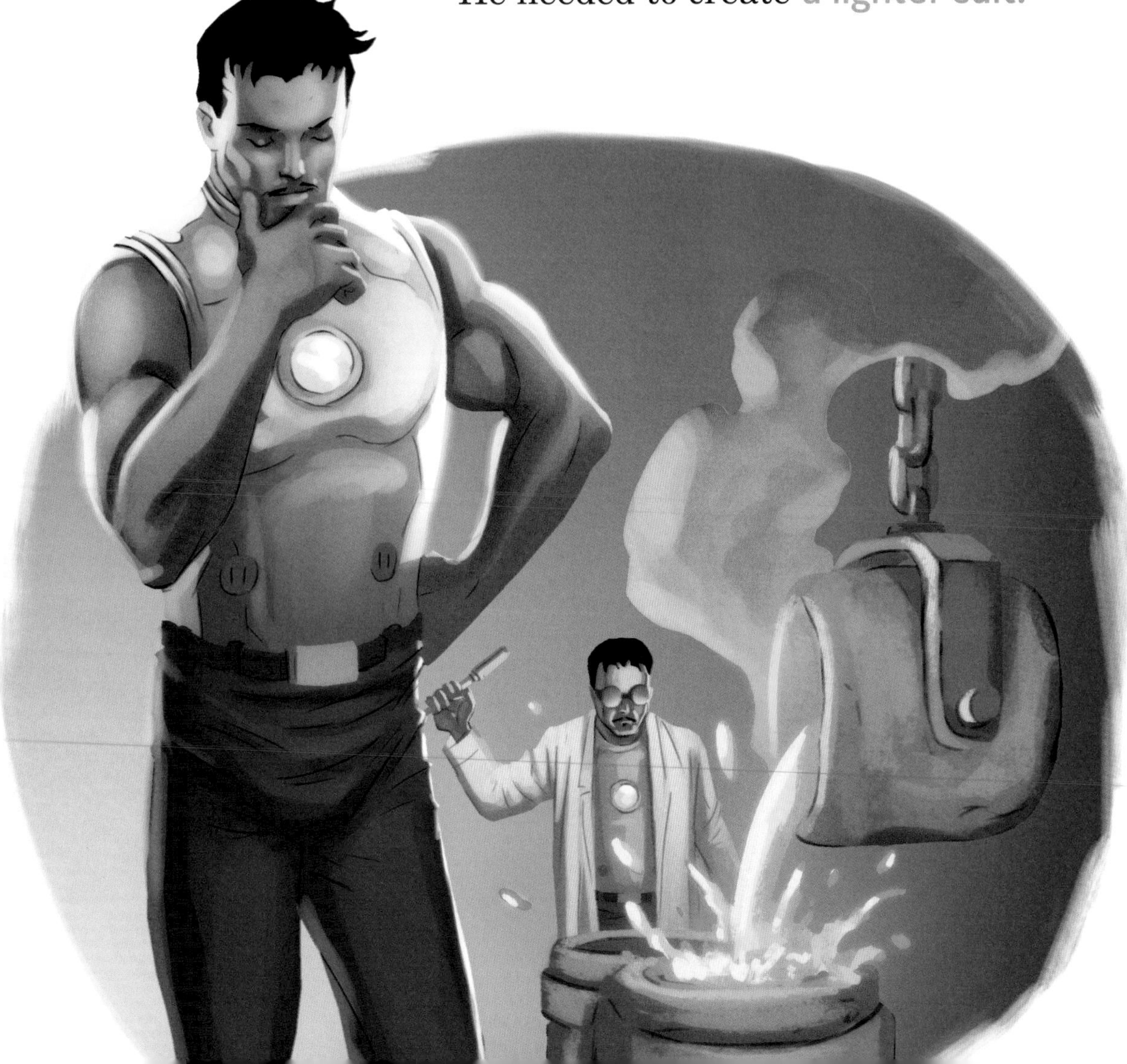

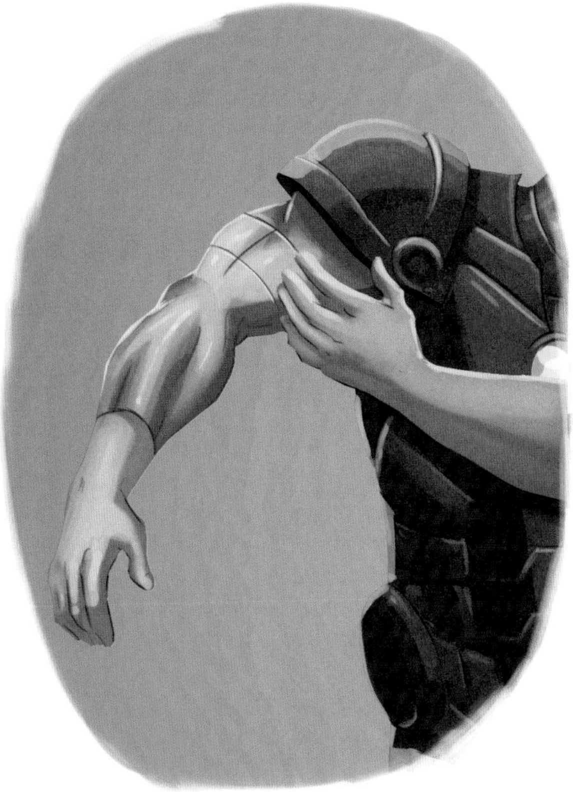

All he needed was for his chest plate to remain attached. Everything else could be changed.

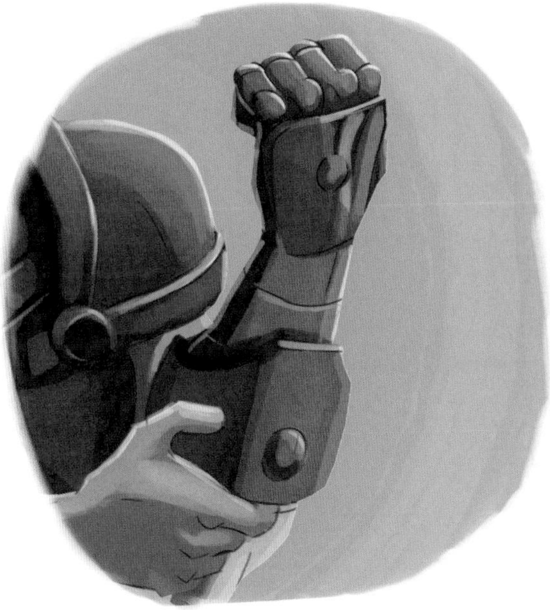

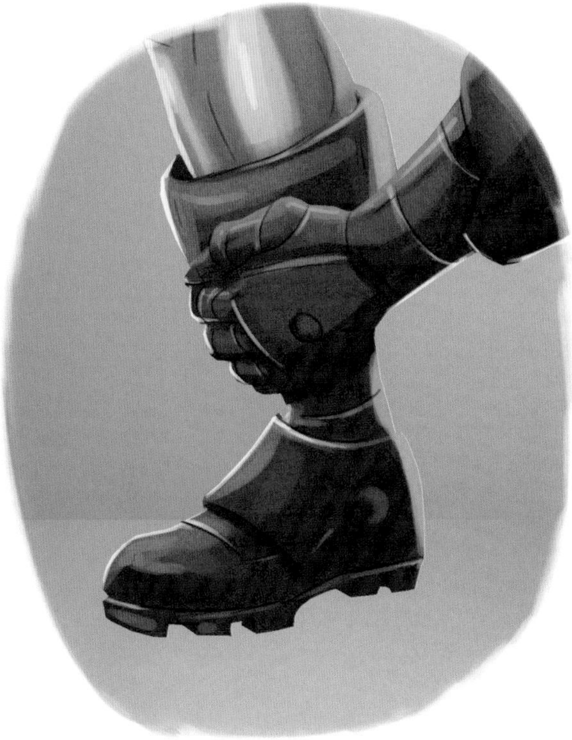

Soon Tony perfected his armor . . .

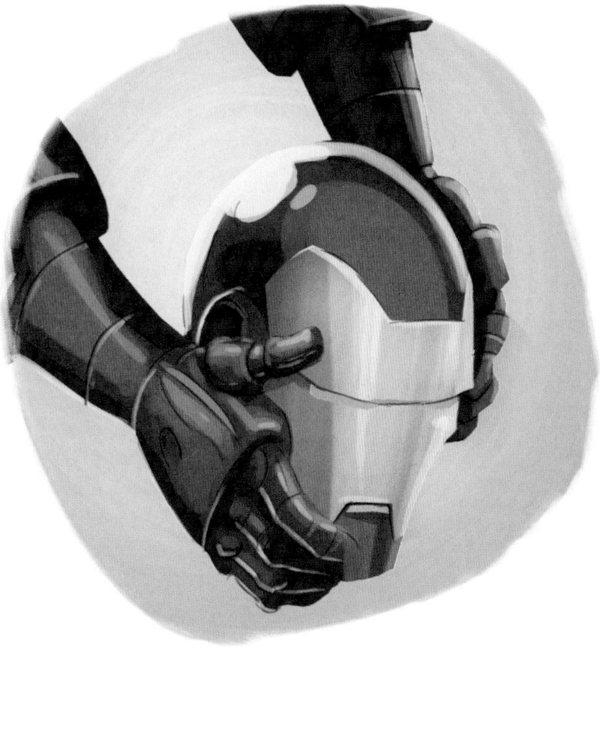

And the Invincible Iron Man was born again!

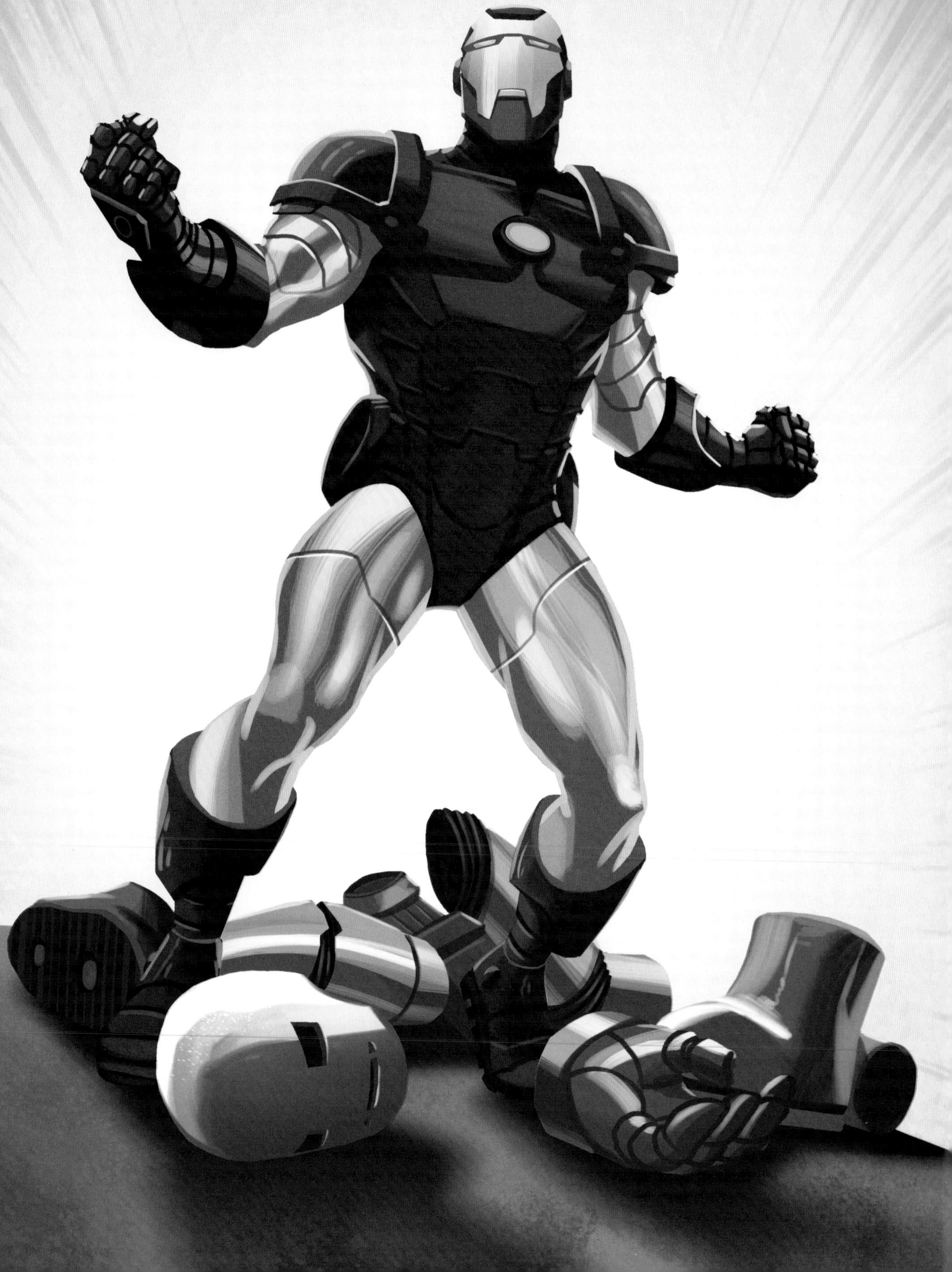

And as Iron Man, Tony never stops **fighting**.

He protects people
at home . . .

. . . and around
the world.

And when he's not fighting for
justice as Iron Man . . .

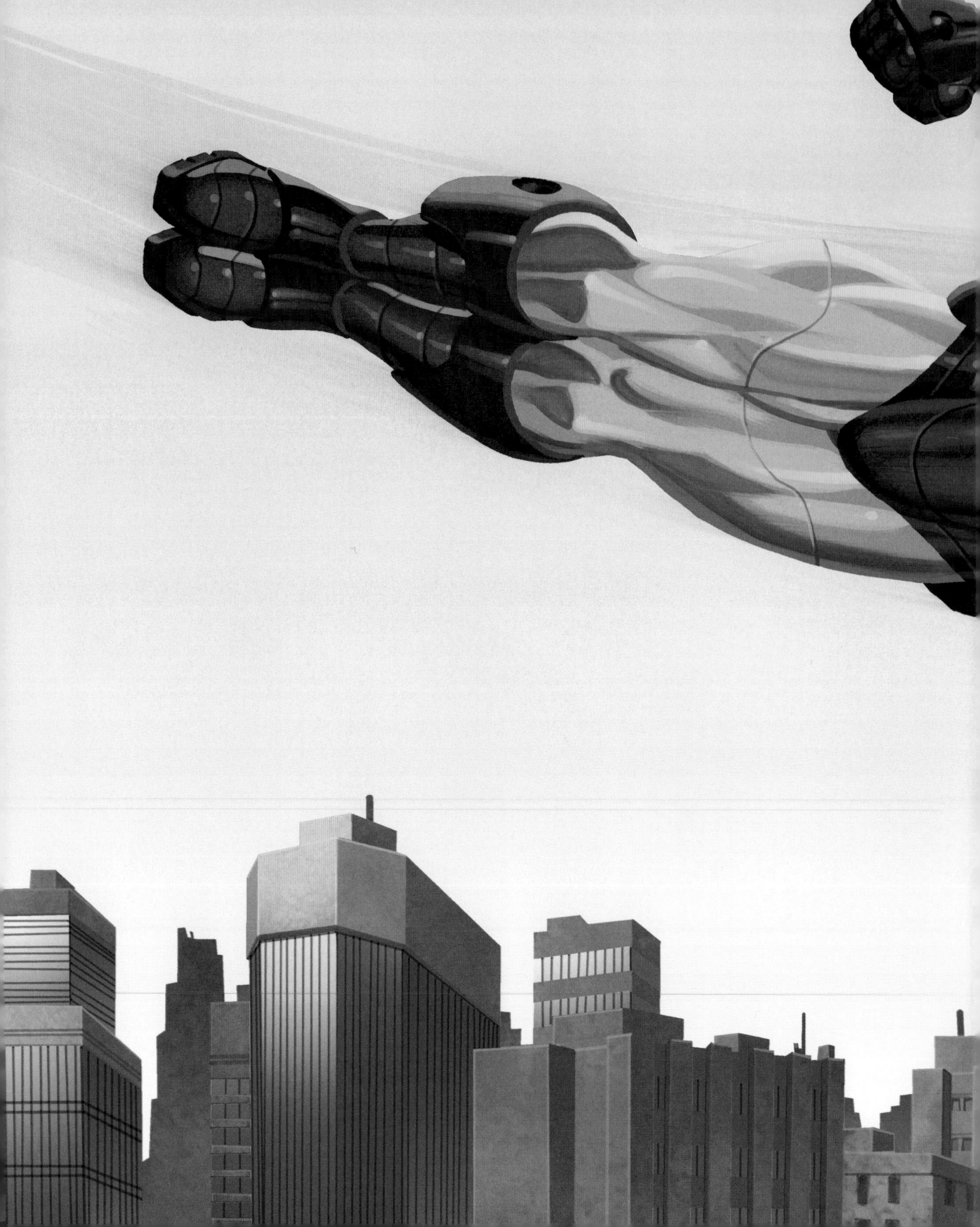

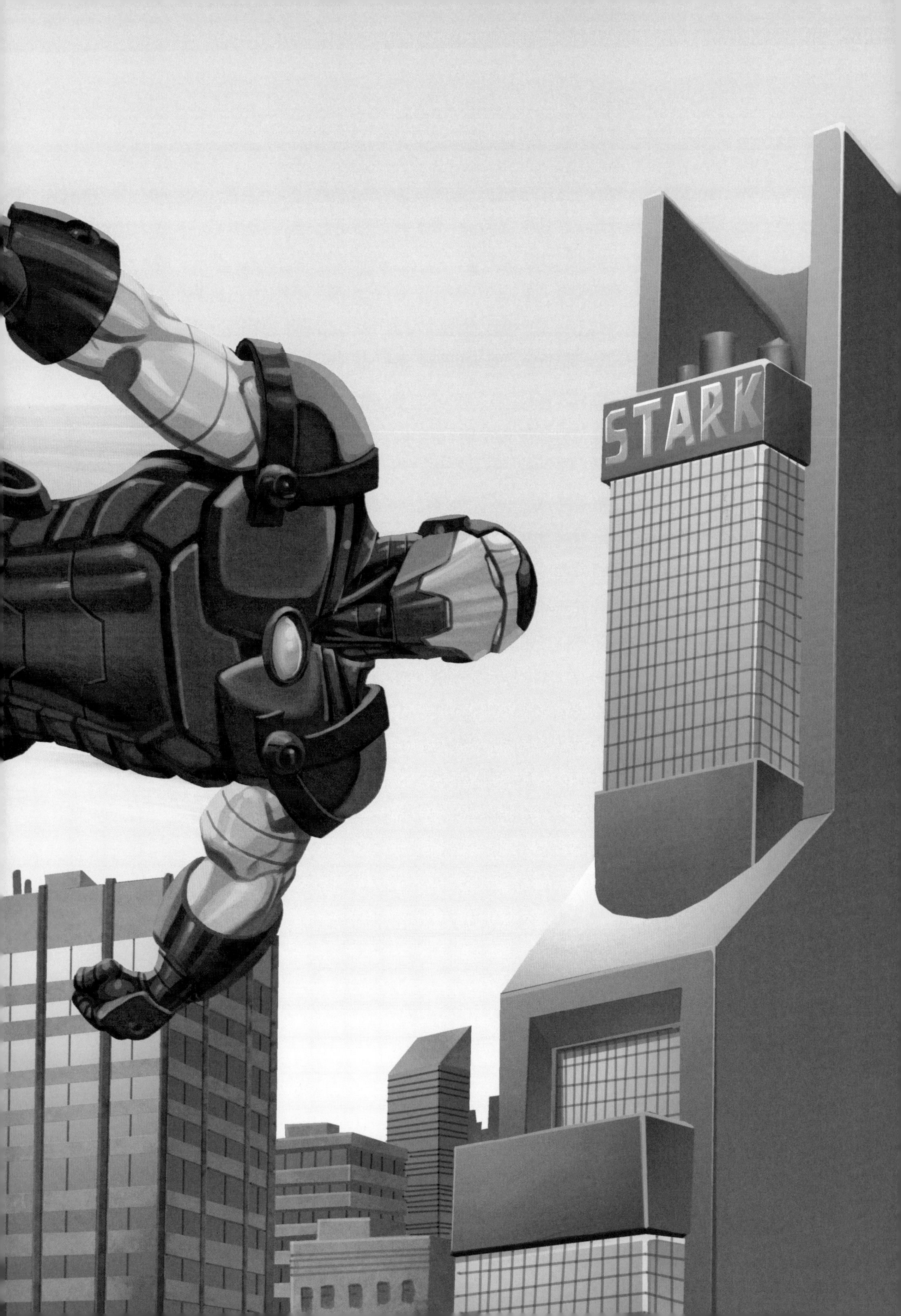
STARK

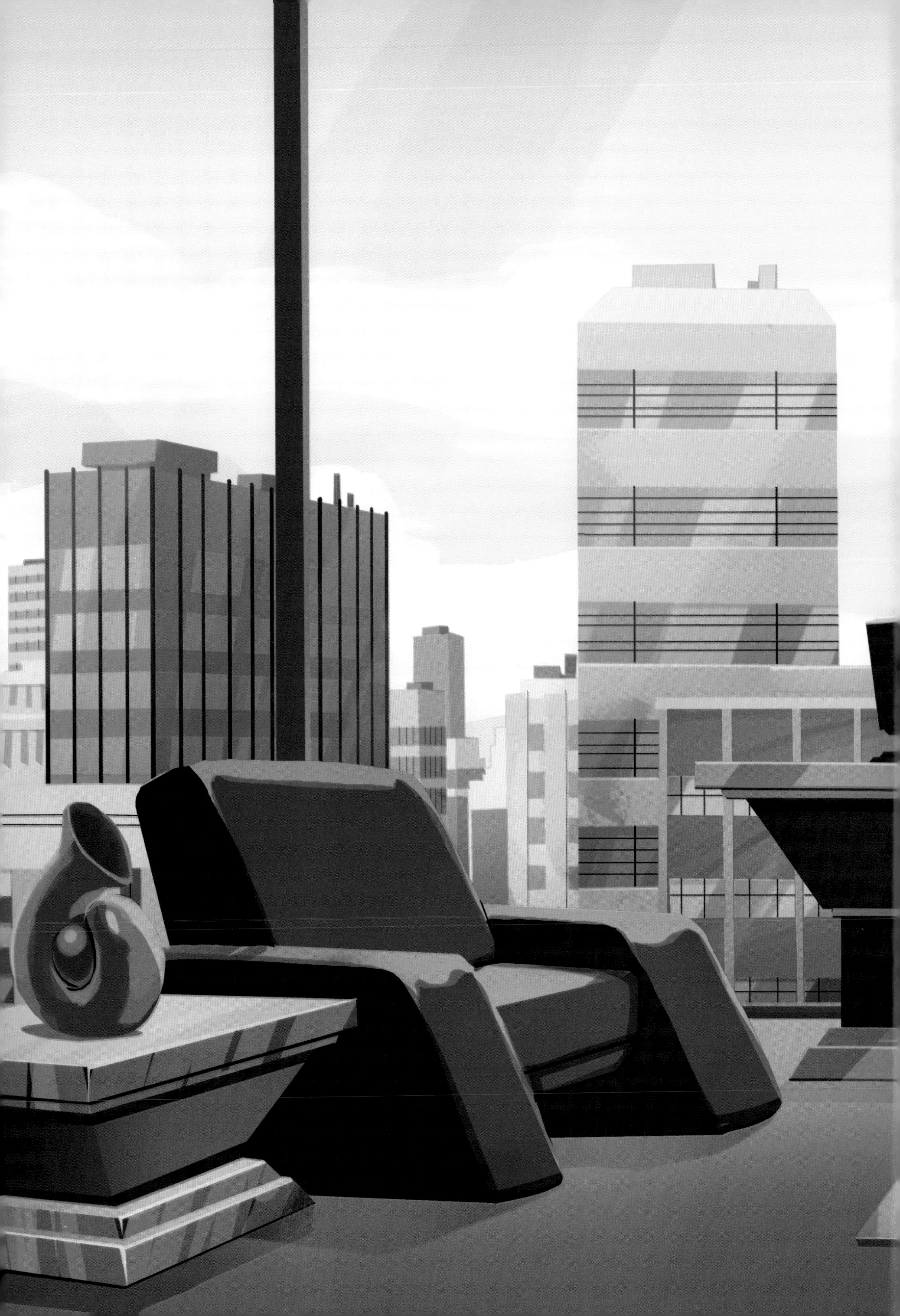

. . . Tony runs his company,
Stark Industries.

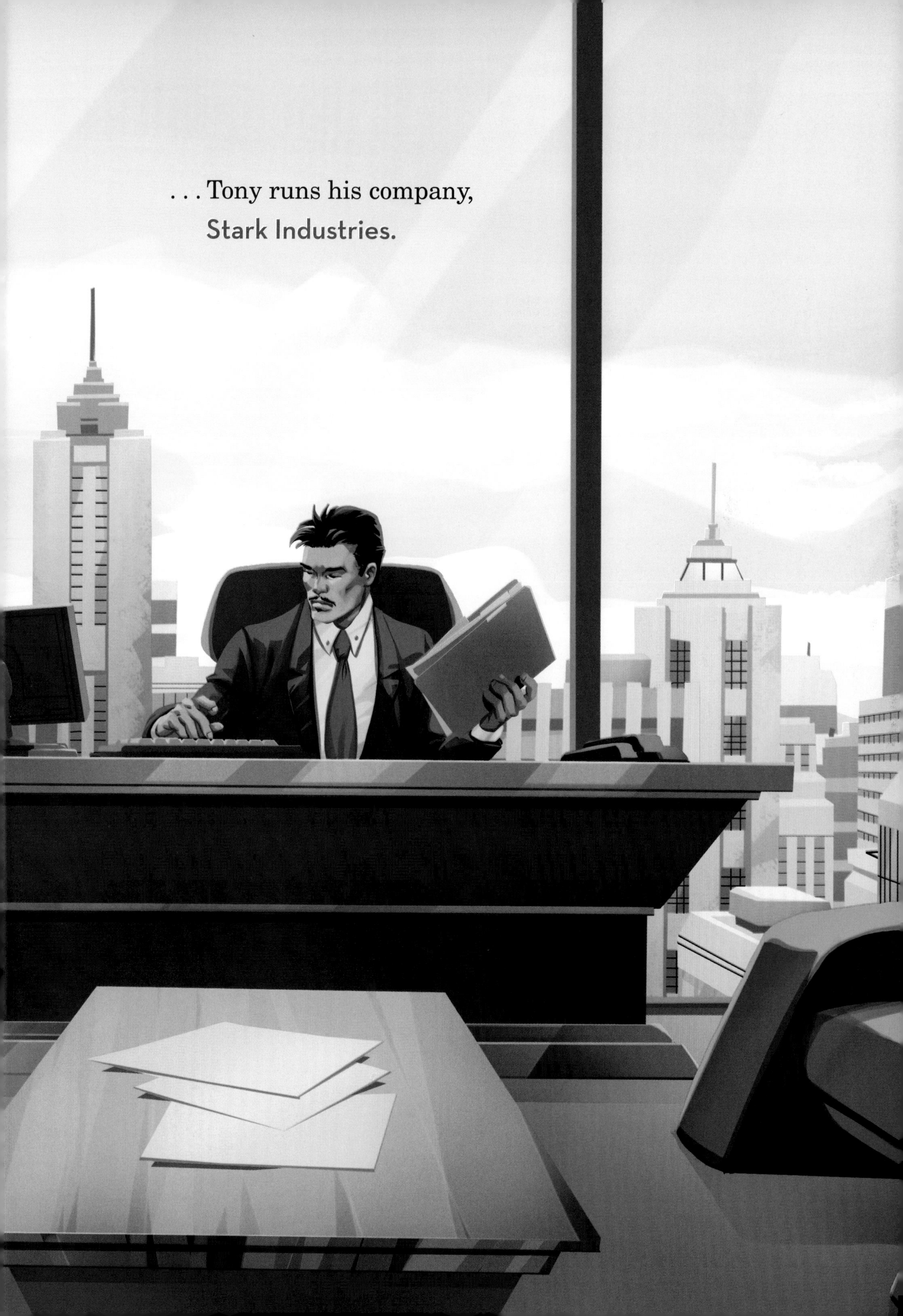

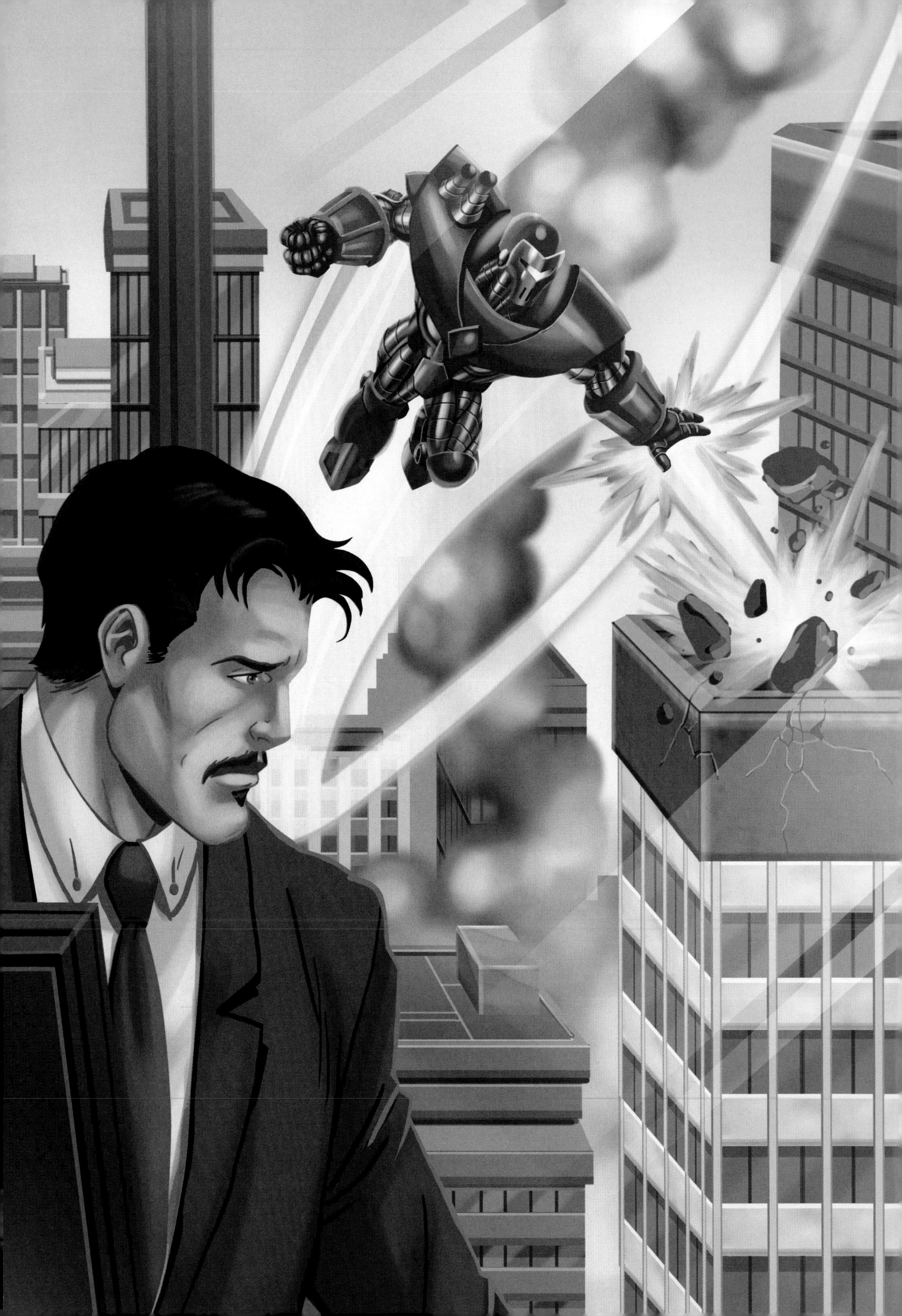

Stark Industries might need
Tony to be a **businessman.**

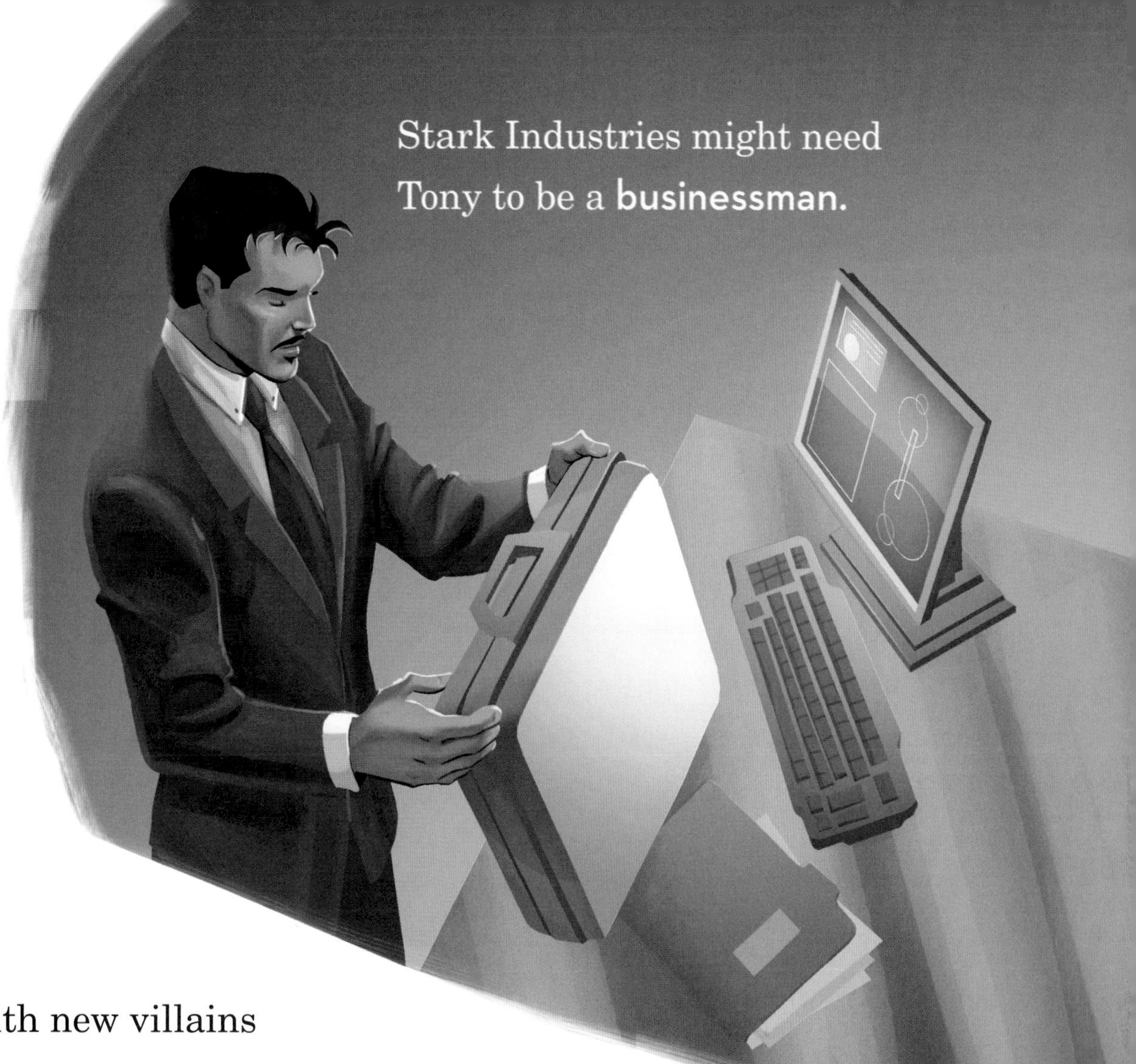

But with new villains
attacking every day,

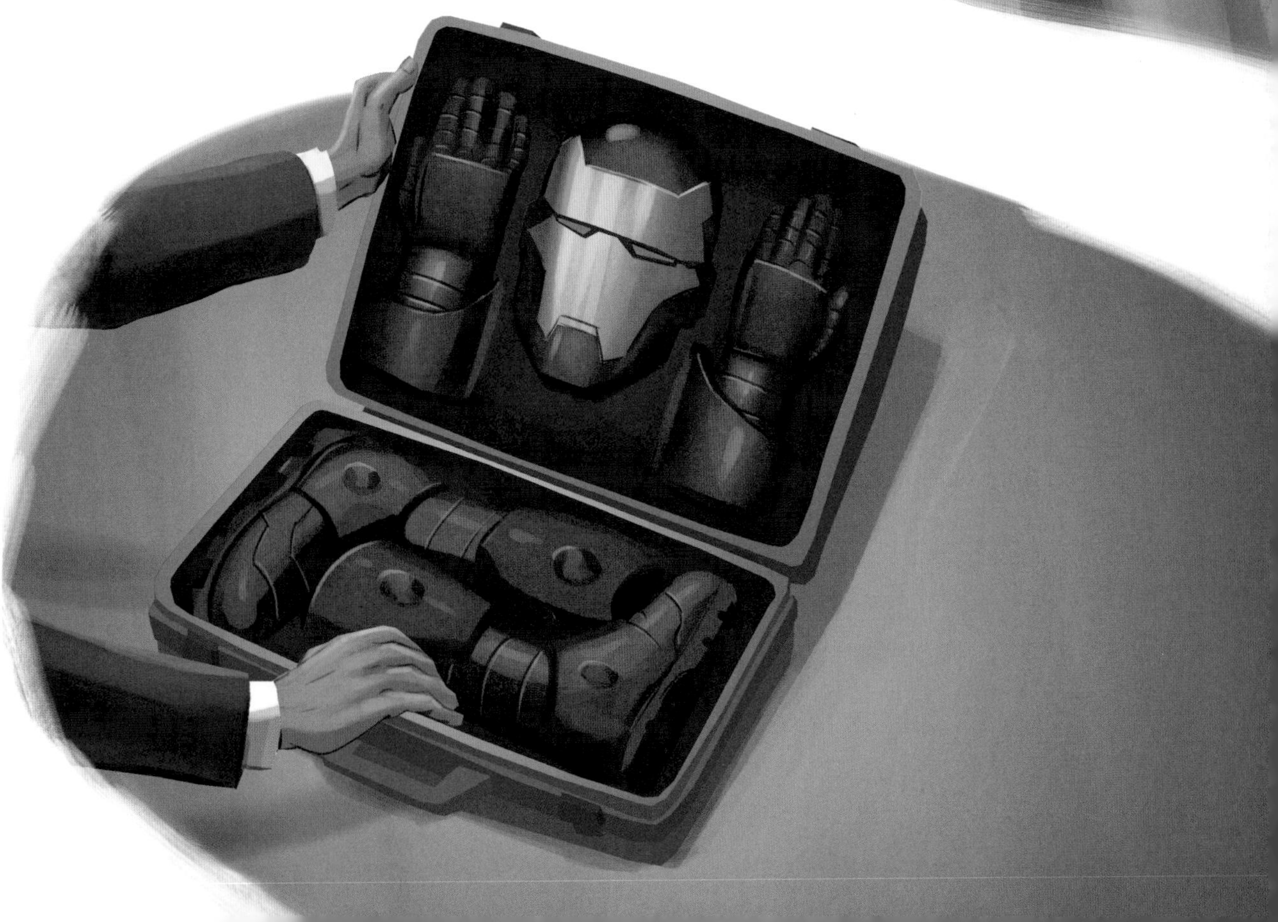

the world needs Tony to be an

IRON MAN!

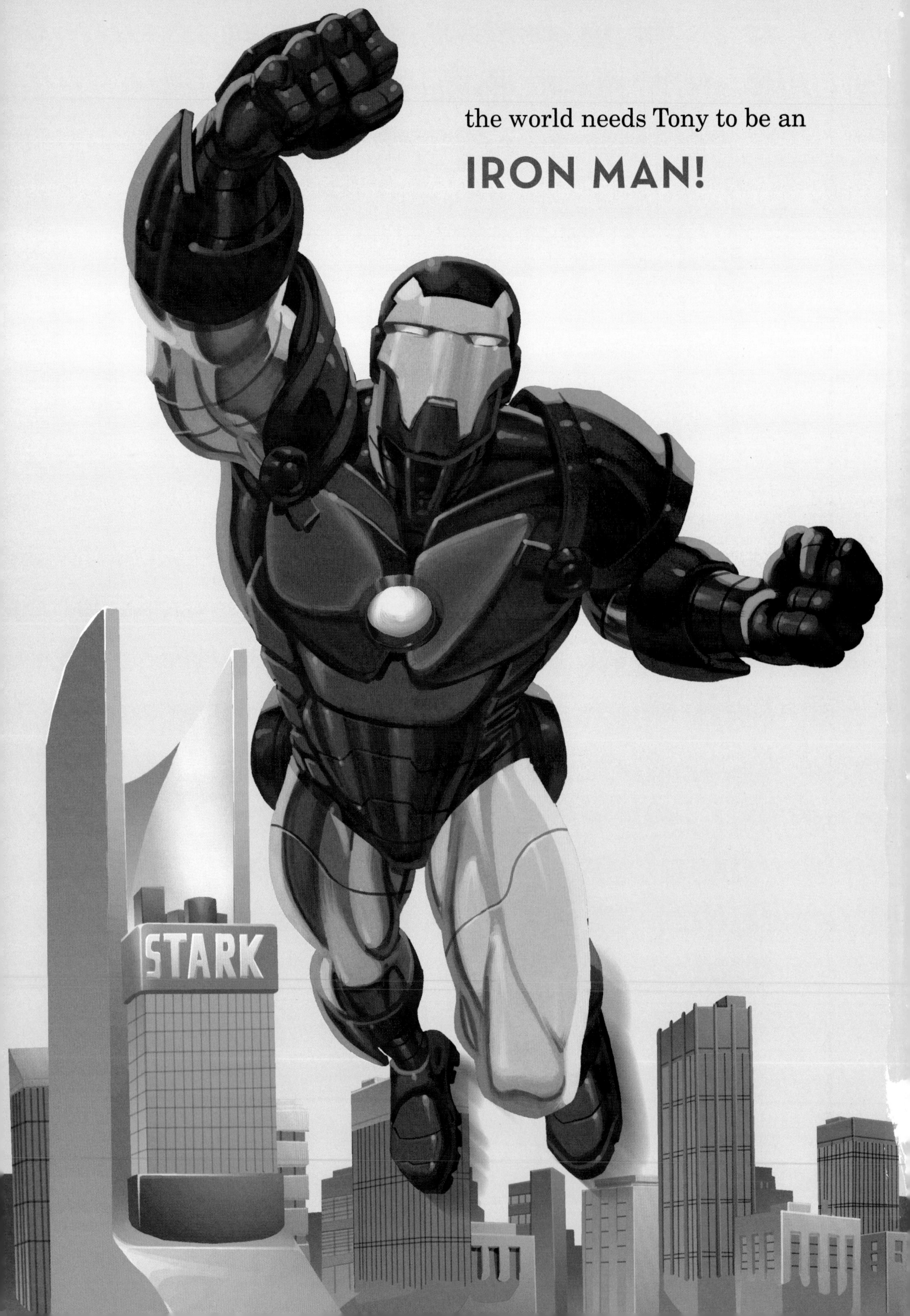
STARK